Wayward

Catherine Clump

Contents

Chapter 1

S ong - Talking Body - Tove Lo.

Picture of our darling Ryan on top as Lucas Till. Got inspired for this after reading Mia Asher's book.

I'm no angel. Far from it. The things I do would make moral people cringe.

I'm the bad guy.

The gold digger.

The side piece.

I don't give a fuck what anyone thinks. I've stopped caring about so many things a long time ago.

"Oh shit. I'm about to cum." Brian groaned before releasing himself into my mouth. Granted I was a bit annoyed that he hadn't taken my advice when I told him to eat a lot of sweets because I didn't need his sour cum in my mouth. But for the sake of it I just let him do it anyway. I still spat it out after he was done.

He moaned lying down "Shit babe that was not hot. Why did you have to spit it out?"

"You know why." I answered getting off the bed still in the nude. Brian's silk sheets caressed my body as I tried to get up.

I walked barefoot to the coffee table where the bottle of the expensive white wine we had opened during dinner.

"Baby come back to bed. You know I only get to see you tonight before I go to Italy tomorrow." Brian whined patting on the empty space beside him.

I drank straight from the bottle and smirked before whipping my mouth with the back of my hand and turning back to face Brian. "And whose fault is that?" I purred.

He groaned again throwing his head back into the pillows. His legs were splayed open revealing his large package. The sight was almost enough to make me want to go back and climb it again. "I wish you could come with me this time. But you've got college and all."

"School comes first." I said absently. He groaned again. I sighed and closed my eyes since all his groaning and moaning started to annoy me. Brian and I had been "dating" for about two months, which was pretty close to my official cut out point so I expected that sooner or later my annoyance would get the best of me and I would end up dropping him.

But that was no problem for me. There was always one opportunity or the other waiting for me. The truth was that I was always and would always be wanted. Call me what you want, a whore or a slut, I don't care really. Those labels have become mine. I wear them proudly. I know what I am and I've embraced it.

I took another swig from the wine bottle before I felt hands creeping around my waist and pulling me towards a very sweaty chest. Disgusted,

I pulled away abruptly "Go take a shower or something. You know I can't stand all that sticky sweat." I said annoyed. I couldn't stand sweat on me or anyone else.

Brian chuckled raising both hands up "Alright, don't get your panties in a twist. Unless you're wearing them again for me."

I rolled my eyes and went back to lie down on the bed leaving Brian to still stand. "I'll think about it if you're good."

I could see his dick twitch again at my words. Goodness, men were so predictable. And that made them so much easier to control.

"Well I almost forgot." Brian said moving to the side of the bed. He brought out a box from under the bed with a familiar label in faint silver on top "I got you this last week. I know it's your thing so I knew you'd like it."

Inside was the Hermes scarf from the latest collection that I had been dying to get. It was featured in this year's Paris Fashion Week and I knew that I had to get it at all costs. A greedy smile brightened up my face as I snatched it up in glee "Oh thanks babe! I've been dying to get this!"

Brian grinned "I knew you'd love it. Consider it my sendoff gift until I return from Italy next week."

I smiled seductively "Then why don't you come and get your gift right now." I spread my legs wide for him to see what I was offering once again.

The sight of his dick shooting up faster than a rocket never got old.

"That's depends.... will you let me top this time?" He asked hopeful.

I pretended to think before shrugging and placing my hands behind my head "Sure. Why not?"

Yeah the thrill of being wanted never got old, no matter what anyone ever.

Chapter 2

Picture of Jay on top as Jacob Artist (he's so cute).

"When will I see you again?" Brian asked as he turned off the roaring engine of his Aston Martin. I shrugged "You'll see me when you see me."

He sighed obviously not happy with my answer "Can't I ever get a straight-forward answer from you?"

I turned to him with an over exaggerated smile "We'll talk when you get back ok?"

Brian decided that that was good enough for him and Frenched me rough-ly before allowed me hop out of his car finally. I waved with a sexy smile before walking into my apartment building. I was greeted by Peter at the Lobby.

"Hey Pete." I greeted pleasantly.

"Hi Ryan guy. What you've been up to?" He asked with his ever mischie-vous smile. I shrugged "Just doing the do like I always do right?"

Peter was a pretty good guy and very easy on the eyes too. But he was sadly a bit below my price range for now. And straight.

He laughed shaking his head while I walked up to the elevators. I reached my two bedroom apartment and tossed my keys into a bowl. My apartment was a lot more expensive than that of the average college student. It was a gift from boyfriend number 3, about 5 boyfriends ago.

I loved and relished it because not many of my peers could boast that they lived in a two million dollar apartment. So maybe I didn't work as hard..... Or I did really when you think about it.

I turned on my voice machine expecting the same series of messages. Just a few acquaintances inviting me for drinks and what not, my best friend Jay reminding me that we had dinner sometime this week. And the last was somewhat expected.

"Hey Ryan. It's Chris calling -"

I deleted it off without listening. I really didn't need to.

Even though I'd showered at Brian's place, I still showered once again before falling right into bed surrounded by my textbooks. Just because I lived a fun life didn't mean that I had to be behind in my work. That was something I would never take for granted.

I studied for about three hours before my droopy eyes and tired body decided that I'd amassed enough information for now. I shoved my books away and I laid my head on the pillow to sleep.

I honestly wasn't always this way. Nor was I always this wanted. There was once a time when my self-esteem didn't reach the top of a frying pan.

In high school I was skinny, unwanted and filled with acne and blemishes. Naturally I was every bully's dream. But there was one particular kid who I hated more than the rest.

"Hey four eyes! Look over here. Or can't you see that?" Nathan Coffey snickered causing his friends to join in the humiliating laughter. My cheeks burned and I wanted to cry so badly. I was such a weak person then. No backbone of my own.

I felt a shove that sent me tumbling to the ground. My glasses fell off my face and skidded on the floor. I couldn't help it. The tears ran and ran.

"Fucking cry baby. Cry all you want. No one cares." He taunted. Everyone who was around either laughed, or stared without helping me. There was no one who actually took pity on me.

He was right; no one cared.

That's right I was bullied. Severely. I don't think back on it and feel sorry for myself. I like to think back on it as the prelude of who I would later become. I didn't mourn those years anymore, but I did make the years after them so much better for myself.

The next morning I sat in my usual coffee shop with my usual order of chai tea and a white chocolate muffin cooling in front of me. My textbook was right in front of me.

"I just need to look for the table with the cutest blonde and the most boring drink order to find you in any coffee shop." I heard a familiar voice teasing me.

I rolled my eyes fondly "Don't let Patrick hear you. He might have my ass."

Jay, my best friend ever, sat on my table with a shit eating grin on his face. "Ohhh studying this early morning. Got a test?"

I met Jay when I first moved to New York. He was my roommate during freshman year and we hit it off immediately. He was there to guide me when I was still new and adjusting to life outside my hometown. He's the second friend I ever made in my life.

I shook my head and sighed "No got my usual study time cut in half last night."

"What happened?" He asked curiously.

I let a small devilish smile reach my lips "Brian happened."

He laughed "And here you are pretending to have hated every second of it."

I sighed dramatically causing him to shake his head. Jay didn't disapprove my lifestyle per say, he just humored the idea that I was delaying the return of my personal Prince Charming into my life by playing around the way I did, which of course I viewed as absolute bull. I didn't blame him; this would be his fifth year anniversary with his boyfriend Patrick who he met on a trip to Australia when he was 17.

So of course he was the perfect example of the few who'd actually gotten lucky enough to find someone compatible with them and then decided that true love was an entity which really existed. I really didn't care much for it, until he'd started trying to enforce his beliefs on me.

"He's not lacking in the bedroom department at least. Which makes up for something, since the man can barely pull his IQ together for anything that isn't partying or bragging." I rolled my eyes.

Jay hummed "Maybe someday you'll find an actual person who doesn't make you want to yawn."

I sighed sipping my tea "Can't help it if I'm a hard-to-please diva."

He rolled his eyes "And maybe then you'll stop this whole 'I'm an ice prince' facade."

"It's not a facade." I said matter-of-factly. "A facade would imply that there's something else I'm hiding and that my current disposition is nothing more than a cover up."

Jay leaned over and looked at my straight "One of these days you're actually going to have to be honest to yourself for once."

"I am being honest with myself. I love my life the way it is. For me there's nothing better than being pampered and getting expensive stuff while also getting occasionally bomb-ass sex on the side. It's my ideal way of living. Just like your ideal way of living is your cute but somewhat exhaustive co-dependency with Patrick. You don't see me criticizing the fact that you guys have a Sushi night every Tuesday but I guess it works for you." I defended. We always had some form or the other of this kind of talk and I usually tried to get out of it to the best of my ability.

Jay sighed a bit "I'm not critizing your way of life. I just think you could so better because isn't this an endless cycle for you? Don't you want something stable?"

"It's not a cycle. It's predictable." I admonished. "It's stable enough for me."

"I'm sorry if I sound like a douche in all of this, but I just really want you to be happy." He said genuinely.

My fingers curled around my Styrofoam cup "I am happy with my life. Very happy. And if comes down to nothing, at least I still have you and Patrick."

He smiled a bit at that "Yeah you do. Just promise me you'll do whatever makes you happy yeah?"

I looked outside "Oh look. We need to get to class now."

Jay didn't say anything but I knew what he was thinking when we gathered our things. He believed in love but I didn't with a good reason not to. I was plenty realistic and honest to myself. Love to me was an urban legend. It was useless for me to chase after something I'd never seen before.

"Do you have a shift today?" I asked Jay once we stepped outside.

"Yeah. It's a pretty late one." Jay replied. He worked at a bar down in the East Village.

"So I'll see you later right?" I asked and he nodded.

"Don't forget we have dinner this week." He warned. "I'll skim your ass if you miss it."

I chuckled "I won't don't worry. I'm sure Patrick is dying to see me."

"He is!" Jay defended making me laugh further.

"He's just keeping me close the way you keep your competition close." I teased.

Jay scoffed "My man ain't got competition from anyone. Even if you do have a hot white ass."

I raised my hands in surrender "You said it not me. See you later."

"Sure thing." Jay replied with a pat on the back.

I turned to leave but Jay being himself called me back when we were about a meter away from each other.

"Hey Ryan!"

I turned to him confused "What?"

"It's fajitas night not sushi night you asshole!"

I couldn't even help my laughter if I wanted to "Noted!"

Chapter 3 (Greendale)

Eye, draw and sink. That was my technique when it came to seduction. Eye your prey and observe his characteristics to know whether he's worth your energy or not. It also makes you know whether you'll only talk for ten minutes, or if a full conversation.

Next, you don't chase after him. Make him chase you. Draw in his attention by making him see in you what everyone else lacks. Give him a reason to meet you across the room and not anyone else.

Finally, you sink him in hard so that he's completely smitten and there's no chance he's going to look for anyone else anytime soon. Charm and entice him subtly, but don't let yourself be perceived as desperate. Make him think that you might be interested in him, but he needs to gain more of your attention. Most men fall for this a lot.

After my reinvention, my confidence had increased drastically and I was no longer the shy eyed nerd everyone knew the previous year. In place of my bulky glasses were now hardly noticeable contact lenses. My acne had been cleared up and only smooth skin remained. Even my baggy clothes had been replaced with designer jeans and shirts.

Over the summer I had gone from something akin to being the ugly duckling to a beautiful swan who was ready to fan the same waters that had rejected me. And I knew exactly who to thank for all of this.

For about two weeks, I had eyed my prey intensely. I knew his movements, habits and interests well enough. I also knew exactly when to make my grand entrance.

"Low fat soy latte please." I asked sweetly to the female barista who didn't seem to care either way of I was being nice or not. But it wasn't her attention I was seeking.

"Funny. That's exactly what I was about to order." A deep voice said beside me.

I turned with a surprised look on my face "Oh, well what a coincidence. Looks like we both have the same tastes in elaborate coffee orders."

He laughed then surveyed me for a moment "Gerard Coffey."

"Ryan Perry."

"Your name sounds familiar. Can't really remember where I heard it from though." Gerard said with a frown. Of course it was familiar. His brother had provably mentioned it more times than I may have liked in the past.

With an exaggerated sigh, I said "It's ok. Not sure really. Maybe I have one of those really common names."

"Well it'll probably come to me soon enough. So are you waiting for someone or would you like to join me?" He offered and I knew that I was drawing him slowly.

"I'm not sure. You look like you were ready for a quiet afternoon and I don't want to spoil that." I said feigning hesitancy.

"Oh no I insist. You're not disturbing anything. I was actually lamenting about having to drink my coffee alone again." Gerard replied with the very same charming smile I was sure ran in the family.

My expression was as though I was considering "Well...alright. But not for too long."

"Of course." Gerald answered quickly. Our conversation would of course take too long, we'd talk about so much at length and at the end he would be sliding me a torn paper with his phone number written down so that we could "hang out" once again.

With the paper curled in my hands, I could feel the very first wisp of victory go through me.

My first attempt at hunting had gone quite better than I expected. The very next week we'd somehow found ourselves at the same coffee shop for several impromptu discussions. By now Gerald had gotten a lot freer with me and talked about practically everything.

By the third date, he'd let subtle hints about his sexuality.

By the fifth date, he'd asked if I was seeing anyone.

The seventh time we met, it wasn't at the coffee shop but at a hotel right in the next town. He was afraid of anyone he knew seeing him there but I assured him that it would be fine. No one would recognize him. He could be free with me. Oh and how free he was.

It was my first time but I hardly cared as I was more engrossed in the passions and sensations which I had never experienced on my own. Gerald definitely fucked the way he lived: hot and entitled in everything he did. When we had both finished, I let him lie for half an hour on top of me with my fingers tangled in his hair while he lay placid like a cat.

He mumbled something about how his girlfriend Cynthia had never let him take her like that. I was too pleased with the news that I neglected to mention a minor detail to him. It didn't matter anyway. My mission had succeeded.

Gerard really had no need knowing that he'd just fucked his little brother's classmate.

Love it? Hate it? Let me know!

Chapter 4

S ONG - FUCKED MY WAY UP TO THE TOP - LANA DEL REY

Today was a job day which meant that there was hardly anything exciting to look forward to. Brian had come in the day before from Italy and my presence was demanded for dinner and very likely a night of coitus. With the classes and work that I had scheduled for today, I honestly wasn't really forward to it.

I worked at a high-end boutique in the Upper East Side. While my many relationships had become a profitable venture for me, I couldn't depend solely on it. My job was both a back-up plan and frontier for new opportunities. The people who frequently visited were wealthy females with their men or simply men who were looking for wares to impress the women in their lives or their mothers or something. They always needed help deciding what clothes or scarves were better for the person they were buying them for. Help that I provided and was usually thanked for.

I couldn't count the number of times I'd been slipped business cards and phone numbers from these "grateful" clients hoping to make my acquaintance soon. So my job remained an asset even if it took a chunk of my schedule. It didn't hurt to keep hunting and looking because opportunities never really ceased in my opinion.

Besides with Brian's current attitude, dropping him wasn't such a distant prospect anymore.

"I'm out for lunch Ryan. Cover the counter for me?" My co-worker Marissa shouted from her station at the checkout counter.

"Of course." I paused. "Where exactly are you getting lunch?"

"The not very pricey Italian place down the road. The one with the really good risotto." She replied making me grimace. I really wanted her to grab something for me but I couldn't afford any unnecessary carbs. With my course load piling up this week, I really couldn't really afford to gym for hours at my apartment's twenty four hour gym.

But at the same time I had already finished munching on the olives I'd brought with me on the subway here and I really didn't feel like rushing to the supermarket about eleven blocks away for a simple jar of olives.

"Want me to grab anything for you?" She offered once I'd gone to the counter.

"Maybe just a chicken Panini and some juice." I replied. Some garlic bread sounded really nice also but I needed to lessen the carbs.

Being beautiful was such hard work.

She gave me thumbs up before disappearing to the back door reserved for employees only. The shop was unusually quiet today. Normally it would be bustling with women clambering around to grab the best and latest deigns before anyone could reach them.

I assumed that there were no parties or gatherings which required new clothes so that women really had no need to shop. But who the hell was the kidding? Women didn't need any real excuses to shop. All they really needed was an unlimited credit card and shops that were open and sold clothes.

Those two were reason enough.

A young woman in her thirties appeared with a man around the same age as her appeared to the counter.

"I'd like to purchase these please." She said dropping two dresses for me to ring up.

"Was your shopping experience up to your satisfaction ma'am?" I asked politely.

Her black and white manicured nails drummed against the counter "Obviously. Could you please ring up my purchase?" She was impatient. It wasn't my fault that Madame Henrique forced all her employees to recite that dumb line to customers after they'd finished shopping.

The man beside her had an inquisitive but leveled look on his face.

"Of course ma'am." I replied.

After confirming that the dresses cost about $4000 each, I asked the lady "Would you like to pay with cash or card?"

Then she proceeded to pat the man on his chest "Darling, pay the boy."

With a sigh I could empathize with, the man produced a black Amex Card which made my fingers tremble just a little. Brian was still at gold.

"You're good to go." I said with a smile handing back the card. His fingers deliberately brushed with mine as he collected it and I could feel his gaze smothering me slightly.

"Perfect." He spoke up for the first time. His voice was deep and raw. I liked it.

"Oh I just forgot, I need shoes to go with them." The woman said with a small laugh to follow. He rose his eyebrows at her "Couldn't you have gotten it all this time?"

"I'm sorry Neil. I really am. But the shoes are also as important as the clothes and it would be a shame to leave with an incomplete outfit." She pleaded giving him a look which I was fairly certain was mostly used during their private hours. Something that I was not interested in at all.

The man – Neil – paused for a moment. I could see that he wanted to look annoyed but wasn't able to find the right way to show it. Finally, he nodded "Of course, wouldn't want you appearing anywhere without a complete outfit."

She kissed him letting a loud smack sound which jittered me only a little "You're the very best Neil." Before rushing up to the back where the shoes and already bossing Rosy, one of the salesgirls to show her whatever she wanted.

"Demanding little thing isn't she?" his voice startled me slightly. I wasn't expecting him to remain. Of course now I knew the real reason he wasn't mad at her for wasting his time.

"I can't really say anything. But I think you might have a thing for demanding people." I replied after a while pretending to look at something on the computer in front of me.

He chuckled "Learnt something about me after a few minutes of meeting? I'm impressed."

I tried to hide my smug smile "I've been told that I'm very observant. I try to make good use of my eyes." Eye your prey.

"Really? Well tell me what else you can see with those brilliant eyes of yours." He said leaning closer to me.

I glanced at his woman who was still very trying on several shoes before looking back at him "Well you're a very patient man but you like to follow a schedule. You were a little annoyed by her action, but now you're curious about something that's got your attention so you're not going to pay much attention to her at the moment." I said drumming my fingers on the counter.

Neil stared at me for a moment "I am curious about something. Care to inform me what you think it is?"

I tried my very best to hide the smirk I knew was coming "I'm sorry. That would ruin the surprise."

He chuckled "I'm very sure. So it looks as though I'll have to take another method."

"And what would that be?" I asked leaning forward, now curious myself.

He was obviously an observant man himself. No visible personality dents that I could see yet. He was also ridiculously handsome with the confidence to show it back to it up properly. I also knew that he was harboring some light feelings of attraction for me already. I knew and it wasn't about a gaydar at all. There's a look a man or woman gives you and you know that they're looking but not in the fleeting way most people you encounter look at you. It's a look which clearly says "I've seen something I'm very interested in."

It's the way a child eyes candy in a store.

And that was how this very man was also eyeing me.

He swiped the pen that lay right beside my hand and retrieved out a card from his suit pocket. He elegantly wrote what I assumed to be his personal digits on the back of the card and handed them both to me "In case you'd like to help me cull in my curiosity."

I smiled "We'll see."

I only looked at the card after he and his girlfriend had left the store. According to the card, his name was Cornelius Verde and he was the president of Ivy Leaf Productions, which after I googled, discovered was a pretty big corporation.

Of course I'd landed a huge catch.

Now the question was whether to go with it or not.

"Hey Ryan? I'm back from my lunch break." I heard Marissa say. She appeared in front of me handing me a bag with my own lunch.

"Thanks. You're a lifesaver Mar." I said collecting the bag and feeling my stomach growl out at the aroma of the delicious Panini's.

"So anything remotely interesting happen?" She asked.

"No nothing really."

"Where the fuck have you been?!" Brian's demanding voice sounded as soon as I stepped into his place. Simultaneously sighing and rolling my eyes, I dropped my stuff on his coffee table.

"I told you I was at work." I said flopping down to one of the low seated "chic" couches that Brian had for whatever reason. His taste in expensive but tacky as hell couches always made me wonder how tasteless he really was. I understand that his family was already pretty rich, but you could still smell the noveaux riche aura all over him.

"And work goes through till 8pm?" He questioned.

I sighed annoyed "Well I had to study at the library. You know I stay late to study sometimes. Now you can continue interrogating as if you care when we both know you really don't or you can come over for me to suck your dick which would lead to more productive results."

I was tired and irritated so frankly, it would be better to get to the good parts so that I could sleep.

Brian eyed me "Fine. But you better make it good since you made me wait a whole fucking hour for you. You know that I hate to be kept waiting."

"Good boy." I muttered under my breath when he began doing exactly as I wanted. Brian yanked his jeans and boxers down to reveal his very hard dick which flopped in my face. I flicked my tongue over his tip just to tease him for a moment before taking it into my mouth.

He moaned and immediately placed his hand roughly at the back of my head to force me harder on his dick. It annoyed me a little but I let it slide. I normally didn't mind about roughness but today I just wasn't very much in the mood.

"Oh yeah babe take that fucking dick." He groaned out.

I moaned around his dick and took it deeper into my mouth. It got slobbery really fast but I still didn't mind because I was starting to get into it.

Brian groaned and thrust into my mouth "Fuck yeah that feels so good. Not gonna last so long."

I hummed around his dick and sucked it harder. My fingernails dug into his ass pushing him deeper into my mouth as the spit dripped on my face before pulling off and whispering "Wanna cum in my mouth?"

"Fuck yeah."

He let out a completely loud groan and held unto my head harder. The thrusts had increased and I knew that he was getting pretty close.

"Fuck." He shouted clutching my throat as he came into my mouth. Relief that I could breathe again went through me when he released my throat front his tight clutch and pulled up his pants. I was wiping my face with a Kleenex I had found on the coffee table and sighed out leaning back on the couch.

"That was a hell of a welcome babe." Brian commented with grin.

"Thanks." I replied flatly.

He frowned at my response "What the hell is wrong with you today?"

"Nothing. Am I not allowed to be tired or anything? I have a fucking life outside of you." I snapped.

He then pulled his handsome face into an ugly sneer "What the fuck is that supposed to mean? You're also fucking other people? Is that it?"

I rolled my eyes not even bothering to answer him. That was, until he forcefully yanked me right off the chair "Who else are you fucking?"

I tore his hands away from me "Don't you ever touch me like that in your fucking life."

"I'll touch you however I want. I own you. I buy your designer clothes, I pay your rent and I let your strut around town like the fucking pricey whore you are!" He shouted in my face.

I only tilted my head to the side "Oh really? Well let me tell you something Brian. You don't fucking own shit. Just because I let you fuck me and buy me shit doesn't mean you own me nor does it give you the right to lay your filthy hands on me. I am my own person and I choose whether or not to fuck your fake ass. You're completely replaceable because I could walk out that door and get ten of you in a snap without even trying."

Taking insults wasn't even something that I placed much effort into. They just rolled off me like warm honey. But placing hands on me in a way that I wasn't ok with was a serious red flag to me. I was no one's ragdoll to rough handle.

"I'm not the fake one you stupid bitch! You're nothing but a whore! A fucking disgusting whore who wouldn't even be able to raise your head up in this city if you weren't spreading your legs round." He spat.

I rolled my eyes not even fazed "I know what I am unlike you. At least I'm not a cowardly little spaz who's afraid of letting his daddy know that he likes cock so that he won't cut off his trust fund. I wonder if you've even so much scratched your poor fiancée ever since the two of you met."

"Get out." Brian said with the reddest face I had ever seen.

I smirked grabbing my bag "Don't flatter yourself darling. I was already leaving. And spare me the lies; we both know you'll miss me when your girlfriend doesn't let you stick it up the ass."

And with that I stormed off without even an accidental glance back, as fierce as could be. I didn't even bother correcting the asshole about paying my rent: he didn't pay my rent. I bought it myself right for cash.

Chapter 5

----

this is mostly just to keep our blood pressures leveled ;) And I missed updating this story so much

----

By the time I reached the Golden Town restaurant, Jay and his boyfriend Patrick were already seated in their usual booth close to the windows. I wasn't by any means late; it's just that those two had an annoying habit of making me feel that I was with the way they constantly popped in early. Patrick was whispering something in Jay's ear when he arrived which was causing the other male to laugh quietly. Being who I was, I decided to mess with them a little.

"Why I never!" I said loudly causing them both to jerk away and a few heads to turn towards our table. Jay had a murderous look on his face while Patrick just smiled and shook his head at my antics.

"Oh hi Ryan, I'd hug you now I'm too busy trying to control the urge to punch you for distracting me from my boyfriends' luscious lips." Was how Jay greeted me.

"At least now the poor boy can breathe." I said sitting down.

"It's ok Ryan. He's just a little testy because he's hungry." Patrick said in that charming Australian accent of his.

"I resent that." Jay said making us all laugh.

The waiter came to hand us our menus "So how's work going Patrick?" normally I tried my best to include Patrick in our conversations and not make him feel like the third wheel like I was prone to doing when Jay and I first became friends. That was why he joked sometimes that I was his competition. Jay just wanted us to get along which we did mostly.

"Work's amazing. My bosses got a look at that new compressor I designed and they said it could go into the next model we're making." Patrick replied excitedly. He worked as an engineer for a large electronics company which produced home appliances and earned a pretty good living. His main inspiration for work as he told me once was to continue working in his dream career and to provide a great life for Jay.

It was quite remarkable to me that he paid part of Jay's college tuition since the boy was kicked out of his parents after he came out of the closet. The other half was from a moderate sum of money left to Jay by his grandma when she died since she was the only one who accepted his sexuality.

Even though I didn't believe in love, it was hard not to admire their complete devotion to each other.

"That sounds awesome. Remind me to ask for a discount with your name the next time I wanna buy a washing machine." I smirked.

He grinned "Noted. So what about you how's life?"

"Life's great I guess. College is an absolute bitch but at least I'm on top of everything." I replied scanning through the menu before finally seeing something that I liked. "Plus I dumped Brian last night."

"Oh seriously? I literally thought he was going to be the one." Jay said with a teasing tone that said he wasn't completely surprised.

I rolled my eyes "Not when that asshole thought it was ok to put his hands on me."

"He did what?" Jay asked alarmed.

"He just rough handled me a little but I knocked some sense back into the idiot." I replied confidently.

"Then I'm glad you broke up with him then. It's never ok for anyone to ever think that they have the right to hit you." Jay said in all seriousness.

"You're right babe." Patrick said softly to him before giving me a smile. Even if they thought that I lived my life a little on the crazy side, they were still very good friends. I'd only ever had one friend in my life that could rival them.

"And that's why I'm paying for dinner tonight." I announced. "The idiot must have forgotten to cancel the credit card he gave me because it's still been working."

"Wow did you use it to get yourself anything?" Jay asked curiously.

I smirked "Just raked up an impressive mileage of about thirty grand at Yves Saint Laurent this morning."

"That's my boy." Jay laughed raising his hand for a high five which I generously returned. By now we were making a little bit of noise but we didn't care. This was our usual place and we were known to leave good tips for the waiters which I was certain they definitely appreciated.

"Good evening sirs are you ready to order now?" the waitress who handed us our menus now came over to take our orders.

The rest of the evening went through as a blur of good food and warm conversations. When our desert came, Patrick excused himself to go to the bathroom. As soon as he left, Jay leaned closer to me "So there's something weird going on with Patrick."

"Oh like what?" I asked curiously digging my fork into the tiramisu on my plate.

"Well he's been taking calls out side of the bedroom when he thinks I'm sleeping." He said playing around with the mug of coffee in his hands.

"So? Maybe he just doesn't want to disturb you." I suggested.

"That's not all. He's been working later hours now." He added with a worried pout.

I shrugged "Jay, he just got promoted. There's bound to be some more workload and responsibility that comes with the new corner office."

"Yeah but he normally calls to say that he's going to be late but lately he just stumbles in at ass 'o' clock without telling me anything sometimes. The only time I even know he's home is when I hear the fridge being searched. And when I do the laundry, I notice that his shirt has a new scent."

I groaned "Oh please don't tell me it's perfume-"

"-Some heavy industrial liquid because it's really strong, like ammonia because it's really strong. When I asked him about it, all he said was that he did some heavy lifting at work. Like when the hell did he start working in the assembly factory? Unless they include now factory work with every promotion they give." Jay said getting me even more confused.

"So it's not perfume? Great, then he's not cheating on you." I said going back to face my dessert.

"Of course I know he's not cheating on me! That's totally out of the question. What I'm worried about is that my Patrick may be...." He paused with a scared look on his face. "May be producing meth!"

If there was any food in my mouth then, I would have spat it out because of the uncontrollable laughter which escaped me. "What?!"

"I'm serious." It was so said because Jay actually did look serious. "That's the only explanation I can come up with."

"Jay, why don't you actually ask your boyfriend what's going on?"

"I tried but he brushed me off immediately. The only reason he would do such a thing is if he was involved in something illegal." Jay concluded. "Even the other day I called to see if we could have lunch but he said that work was crushing him. Then I called his secretary Jenny and she said that he left the office a little while before I called."

I resisted the urge to roll my eyes "And so you think that Patrick is some sort of drug lord? Patrick, who went to that party a year ago and refused to drink any punch because he thought that it had ecstasy in it? Or the same guy who has never drank a beer in his life? Or are we talking about your angel of a boyfriend who whenever we go clubbing orders a virgin everything, so much that if you told me you guys have never had sex I would totally believe you? I'm pretty sure that doctors would envy his liver and lungs because it must be the epitome of healthy. The only reason he drinks wine is because you force him and I have never even seen him drink more than one glass in all the time I've known you two. So that Patrick is the same guy you think is some drug lord?"

"Hey I've seen Breaking Bad. It's always the people you least expect." Jay argued. "Or maybe that's it, oh my gosh what if my baby has some life threatening disease and is starting a meth empire as part of a bucket list thing?!"

I made sure that my water was quarter filled before dumping it on him.

"Ryan!"

"Cut it out Jay. You're overreacting. I'm sure that there's a very legal explanation for all of this and if you just wait for Patrick to explain it all to you, this whole thing will be cleared." I said patiently hoping that he would get my point.

"I just want him to be ok." He said quietly.

"I'm sure he is." I assured.

"What are you two gossiping about?" Patrick said when he came back with an unsuspecting smile on his face.

"Just naming the top 100 cute boys ever." Jay said immediately with a smile. He was always a quick thinker.

"Awww hope I'm somewhere there too." Patrick pretended to pout. Jay kissed him "Of course, you're number one."

"Yeah I kind of don't want to puke on this delicious tiramisu...." I started but Jay gave me a dirty look which caused me to smile.

I didn't believe in love, but these two were too damn entertaining to watch.

Just out of curiosity, how do you guys imagine me? Do you think I'm male or female (that one's obvious), black, Jewish, Indian, Vietnamese, white etc? It just occurred to me that I wonder how most Wattpad writers who don't state anything about themselves specifically are and I wondered if you guys do too?

(I'll understand if I'm not special enough for anyone to wonder lol).

Chapter 6

━

Here's Jason! P.S Do you guys think that any of my stories is good enough to enter the Watty's or get featured?

I had been with Cornelius's business card for about three days but I didn't make a single move to call him for about two reasons. One, I wasn't quite sure what to think of him yet. Sure I'd observed him in the boutique that day and done my research on Google and tabloid papers to know exactly how his company was doing and to find whatever snippets of his personal life could tell me whether he'd been in any scandals and such. What I had found was a bit satisfying, but it wasn't enough.

Two, I needed it to breathe a little. Calling him immediately would make me seem desperate or in a hurry which was the last impression I wanted impose. Ignoring it for a while made it appear as though he was the last thing on my mind and would possible make him desperate enough to see me if he really wanted to.

For now, I didn't worry about anything.

My classes ended around eleven and I didn't have work so I decided to take care of myself and clean out my apartment. A cleaning service used to come around twice a week but I cancelled it after two weeks because it felt useless and expensive. I was quite capable of cleaning my own apartment myself; I wasn't a completely spoiled brat. Plus it felt a lot better cleaning my house the way I preferred to do it than having someone else do it.

After tossing away old pizza boxes and take out packets, rearranging my bathroom cabinet and spraying Frebreeze all over my apartment, I decided to treat myself to something far all my hard work.

I took a taxi down to Soho where I knew a great Mexican place. This wasn't a usual habit for me though since I had to discipline myself to maintain my great shape. During my younger years, I'd been a fatty. Losing all that baby fat and weight wasn't easy at all so gaining any was a strict taboo in my book.

Even now a small sense of guilt crept right into me when I took a bite of my deliciously crisp taco. Jay normally told me that I was too hard on myself when it came to my weight and appearance, but he didn't understand that it was better this way. The person I was in my earlier teenage years was someone I hoped never to become again. Riddled with doubts, pain, fear, rejection and utter unhappiness. My past wasn't a story I eagerly shared to everyone.

Jay had no real idea.

All he knew was that I was quite unhappy and ran away from home to the minute I got accepted into college.

The only people who knew the other me where those back home. Those who I left behind and those who I hurt before leaving them behind.

Did I regret it the small trail of destruction in my wake?

Absolutely not.

I regret nothing.

It was only fair for me to leave that town which only caused me heartache right from when I was born till I couldn't take it anymore. My family may have thought that my decision was selfish but for the first time then, I was actually doing something I wanted and taking care of myself.

I was only up to the third bite of my deliciously crisp and warm taco when I got bumped into. It fell from my hand and right unto my navy blue shirt which unleashed a string of swear words from my lips. "What the fuck?! Are you out of your fucking mind?!"

The perpetrator looked grossly apologetic "Oh my gosh, I am so so sorry. I wasn't looking at where I was walking at all."

"Damn right." I muttered angrily trying to wipe my shirt with the napkin in my hand and also mourning the loss of my now abandoned taco on the ground. "I really liked this shirt."

"I will happily get a new one right away." He said quickly. "It's the least I can do."

I narrowed my eyes "It was $600 and I got it at Barney's."

His eyes widened "Wow. Then I will happily pay for the dry cleaning because that is way out of my price range."

I sighed knowing that anger wouldn't get me anywhere "It's ok. Was an accident anyway."

"No it's not ok. If I wasn't such a klutz and actually paid attention when I walk, this wouldn't happen." He said shaking his head at himself. "I'm really sorry, let me help."

He wiped my shirt with a napkin I didn't even notice him holding and then took the time to observe his features. He was quite blonde, nice eyes which were a lovely shade of hazel, and a clear handsome face which I admitted grudgingly within me. He wore a messenger bag also and I noticed that there were a lot of stickers of phrases like Paris and Catch me! with pictures of horses and landscapes. It seemed rather unusual and quite adorable for a grown man. He must have a thing for the outdoors.

"Thanks." I said when the stains were only faint now that he had gotten most of it out but it still seemed unlikely that I would ever get to wear it again. "I'm sorry I yelled at you."

"No I should be the one apologizing. I was in such a rush and I knocked you over carelessly." He apologized once again. Normally I would have dragged this out just for the sheer annoyance of it, but seeing how sorry the guy appeared to be, I decided to be civil about this one just once.

"At least you did apologize for it. A typical New Yorker would probably give me a stink eye before walking away." I said tossing what was left of my lunch into the nearest bin. "So I'd give you half a seal of my approval."

"Good thing I'm not a real New Yorker. Only been here for about two years." He said with a shy smile.

"Half lucky me then." I replied with a faint smile of my own. He ran his hand over his head nervously, which caught me as a very attractive gesture "Um, how about you come up to my apartment which is just a few blocks away while I give you a change of clothes before I send your soiled ones to the dry cleaner? It's the least I can do, especially if you have somewhere to be and wouldn't like to show up covered in taco sauce."

I tilted my head a little "I don't have anywhere to go luckily. But I'm not sure it's safe to go up alone to an apartment with a man I don't know who could have lots of pretty girl's heads stored in his refrigerator. That's just the highlight of every slasher movie blonde character.

He laughed "No need to worry about that. Look I'll leave me windows open so that worst case scenario, you'll be able to jump out if anything happens which I doubt it will. I'm the kind of guy who gets faint if I cut my finger or something so violence of my kind is quite a struggle for me." A very handsome one too.

"So you promise to leave the window open?" I asked to be sure.

He raised up both hands "I swear I will. Plus my walls are pretty thin so if you yell lots of people would probably hear you."

"For a serial killer you aren't very good if you're giving your victims the safety routes." I joked.

He played along shrugging his shoulders "It's totally my fault. I spaced out a lot in class and ended up failing criminal school. Principal Ted Bundy said I'd never make it in the criminal world." This actually got me to laugh again without meaning to.

He had a good sense of humor. Quite rare.

"And another thing, I'd like to know the name of my potential kidnapper." I stated.

He smiled "My name's Jason."

"Jason." I repeated back drawing it a little.

With a little deliberation on my path, I agreed to go up to his apartment with him because my shirt felt slightly uncomfortable and the sauce was now sticking to my bare skin. Jason really did live a few blocks from the restaurant. He lived in a decent apartment complex and we went up unto the third floor before my legs got tired already due to the lack of an elevator.

We got up to the fifth floor before Jason reached his apartment. He was silent all through and only made noise when taking out his keys from his bag. It was then I saw the large professional camera sitting in his bag.

"Sorry if it's a little messy. I was in kind of a rush as you already know." He quickly said as if to make up for the state I would find it in already.

"That's ok." I said with a strained smile already preparing to find dirty underwear strewn all over the place and pizza boxes stacked up in a corner. To my utter surprise, it was neater than I expected. The couch, the medium sized TV and everything else was in perfect order. And was that jasmine air freshener in the room?

The only sign of a mess visible was the stack of papers scattered over the coffee table in complete disarray along with a printer next to them and half a cup of coffee.

"If this is your definition of dirty then I don't even want to know what you think of sparkling clean." I said honestly.

Jason shrugged "My mom taught me to keep stuff in order at all times. It's now a terrible habit."

"Ha! This is far from terrible. Half of the men in this city should take cleaning lessons from you."

He blushed a little at my praise "Thanks." He dropped his bag on the floor next to the coffee table "I'll be right back with a shirt for you." And true to his word, he opened his windows before departing to where I assumed was his bedroom.

I sat on the brown comfy couch to wait. His apartment was quite small, but well lived in. Unlike most of the places I was used to nowadays, it wasn't all huge rooms which echoed unnecessarily and filled with modern but tasteless furniture and million dollar minimalist paintings without meaning. It was obviously smaller, but it only made it feel cozier. It was really nice.

Jason had a lot of photos hung on the wall. Photos of people I assumed were his friends and family, some pictures overlooking the city and some other places I didn't recognize. They had to be taken by a pretty talented photographer. There were a lot of outdoor pictures too.

"Got a shirt for you. Well the only one of mine I think might be your size." He said coming out of his bedroom and bringing me out of my reverie.

"You're a photographer right?" I replied instead without taking my eyes away from the pictures. Jason followed my line of sight and saw me looking at the pictures. He nodded "Amateur one."

"Shut up." I said. "What I'm seeing is far from amateur. They're really good."

He grinned "Thanks a lot. Been taking pictures since I was fifteen. How did you even know that I'm a photographer?"

"Easy observation. You were carrying a professional camera in your bag which you seemed quite protective of and you have quite a lot of photos on wall which were all shot by you I assume."

Jason smiled "Nice observation. But how do you know it was my camera and my pictures?"

I shrugged "You most of the pictures were taken outdoors and from what I gathered you seem to have a thing for the outdoors with all the stickers of plains and horses on your bag. And have a printer and a stack of glossy paper scattered around your table which can be used to print a few pictures if you take them yourself. My other theory is that you have a roommate or significant other who you share this place with and takes their work very seriously. And might make you carry around their camera for some reason."

"Anyone ever tell you that you have really observant eyes?" He asked moving closer.

I smiled a little proud "A few times maybe."

"I don't have a roommate or sadly a significant other like you said. Not like it's every day I get to bump into cute guys and spill food on them." Then his eyes widened after realizing what he had just said. "Oh shit, I'm so sorry! Not everyone likes that and-"

I laughed to put him at ease "It's ok I swear. I'm one of the people who are fine with that I guess. Plus it would be pretty hypocritical of me, since I adore compliments." I assumed that he understood what I was implying.

He smiled before handing me the shirt in his hand "So sorry if it's a literal downgrade from your nice shirt but it's all I have out of the hamper and is your size for now. Gonna sort my washing tomorrow."

It was a Yankees t-shirt which made me smile. It was literally the first game I ever saw when I moved to the city. Granted, it was with a handsy diplomat who didn't let me get much of a view since his only objective was to suck hickies into my neck and block my view even though we were watching from the best seats in the stadium. Jay was sick that day which was why he didn't come. Still, it was a great as ever because it was the first live game I saw in New York City.

"It's ok. I'm a Yankees fan so you're safe." I teased.

Jason wiped some imaginary sweat from his brow "Phew, thank goodness. I almost picked the Patriots shirt hanging next to this one."

I laughed unbuttoning my shirt to wear the one given to me. When I was shirtless, Jason awkwardly looked away as if he didn't know if I would be offended or not by him looking at my chest. It was thoughtful to me. Especially when I had been around too many guys not even ashamed to blatantly check me out most times.

"It's funny." He said once I'd worn the Yankee's shirt.

"What's funny?" I asked tossing my own shirt on the couch.

"I've spilled sauce on you, taken you up to my apartment and unknowingly revealed my profession to you yet I don't even have the simple pleasure of knowing your name." he replied.

I remained silent for a little while "Ryan. My name's Ryan."

"Great to meet you Ryan." He said stretching out his hand to me. It took me an embarrassing three seconds to realize that it was for a handshake. "You too."

"Would it be ok with you if I got your number?" He asked seeming a little nervous. I cocked an eyebrow "My number?"

"So that I can call to return your shirt when I've got it dry-cleaned." Jason replied quickly as though he was afraid I would get offended or something. "Unless you'd just like me to leave it on a bench in the Central Park on a certain time and date like in the perfect exchange. That would totally work too."

"No my number is fine. Some hobo might come take it from the bench anyway." I replied grinning. He handed me his unlocked phone where I typed in my number before handing it back. He gave me missed call so that I could also save his own number.

"There. I'll see you when you come by." I said ready to leave. "I'm going to get myself another taco now."

"I'd totally take you but I have to reschedule my appointment since I'm late anyway." Jason said walking with me to the door.

"Oh yeah your appointment." I felt a little guilty since I'd been mad at him when he also had his own urgent thing to get back to. "I'm so sorry you missed that because of me."

"No worries. Everything was totally my fault anyway." He said with a genuine smile. "Besides, you weren't bad company at all."

And I smiled back before leaving the apartment wondering what the hell just happened.

I love your faces. Especially you.

Chapter 7

-------------------Loved the positive feedback from the last chapter. Y'all are awesome. Enjoy the product of my late nights. I update this story every Monday now that I've got my updating schedule up. For my other stories you should check my profile.

SONG - CODES - ELLIE GOULDING

Vulnerability.

I absolutely hated that word. Leaving a part of yourself weak for others to get an easy pass the prey was as terrible as suicide to me. In a way it was the same thing, because once you leave even the smallest opening of weakness for anyone to take a peek, that's a gunshot to the head.

That's death.

And I had died my own death plenty of times before. With shoves and pushes and insults that burned down to the very core of myself. The words were much more painful than even the hits and bruises. At least with just beatings, it only reached the surface of my body and that pain would slowly fade away. But with words, they were made to reach the very nooks and crannies of your being. To tear you from the inside right out.

Like when I was younger, Nathan Coffey's words tore me down plenty. It was quite understandable, he was my bully. He made my life miserable because I was slightly overweight and ugly. His family was rich and that made him entitled to a lot of things I wasn't then so I was his favorite victim for being the opposite of him. I got that loud and clear.

But the person whose words hurt the most was my brother Chris. His insults were the ones I didn't understand. His motive for causing me pain was never clear. But it was the one that made the most impact. He never touched me or shoved me around like the guys in school, but every day he didn't miss a beat when it came to making me miserable or hating myself.

Little things like "Watch where you're going lardo." Or "Where's the last ice cream? You probably ate it all you little fat faggot." Tore off little pieces of me every single time. His hatred didn't make sense to me. I was his brother. Weren't brother's supposed to care about each other? Why did mine hate me? The answer was actually pretty clear but to me it still didn't make sense to my then child-like mind. My brother hated me because I was a little overweight and didn't lift weights like the guys on the football team. Because I was a geek with no friends at all. Because I embarrassed him in school when Nathan Coffey taunted me. Because he was always known as the little brother of the fat ass faggot.

In his right he was a pretty cool guy. He was just in the eighth grade when I was junior. It was even so much more painful because it was my little brother who sent crude insults my way each day. At first I didn't blame him; I ruined his reputation as soon as he entered high school. Instead of a nice clean slate he was labeled as the brother of a freak. But why hadn't he noticed that it hurt me a lot more than it hurt him? That I felt guilty for ruining someone else as well as myself? Why didn't he see that? Why was he so bent on hating me?

After the summer had passed and I was transformed, he was the one that was the shocked the most. My parents who had continually comforted me all those times I came home with tears in my eyes and bruises on my skin didn't know how to take it. All they knew was that I'd taken a trip and come back so much more different than the glasses-wearing, slightly pudgy son they knew and loved all the same. The one who had come in his place was more confident, smiled more and had a certain glint in his eyes they really couldn't put their finger on. It was happiness, finally. He was finally happy.

And as for Chris, well he must have hated me more because the only ammunition he ever had to blame me for anything was gone for good. He'd felt so much better than me then.

Now, he hated himself because it was so much clearer that he wasn't. He'd never been better at all.

"Hi, this is Ryan Perry. You know what to do after the beep." There was a beep. My brother's gruff voice sounded from the answering machine. "Look Ryan, you haven't picked any of my calls in forever. It's not fair. You'd talk to Mom and Dad but you haven't talked me to me. I'm starting to think that-"

I promptly deleted the message before it could continue. My actions seemed cruel but I saw it as self-preservation. I was preserving myself from all the pain and dread filled in my former life and Chris was one of the benefactors of that pain.

"This message has been deleted." The electronic voice informed me.

There would be no more openings.

No more vulnerability.

No more deaths to die again.

"So you're going down to Soho to meet a guy who bumped into you and spilled your lunch all over your expensive shirt because he promised to have it dry cleaned and sent back to you while you return his Yankees shirt you borrowed?" Jay asked me over the phone.

"For the last time. Yes." I deadpanned looking outside the window.

There was some rustling in the background "Babe! You better come say something now to Ryan because it might be the last chance you'll ever get since he's going to get killed at some guy who could be a crazy psychopath's house."

I laughed "Jay I'm not going to get killed. And he's not a killer."

"How do you know huh? Do you have a copy of his birth certificate, high school record, juvie records and psych evaluations?" He demanded.

I rolled my eyes so hard "No. Because I don't need to have all those crazy things to know and I'm not a stalker. Plus I highly doubt he has a juvie record, I've seen his apartment it's cuter than you."

"Hey!" My best friend protested.

"Babe who's the cutest?" I heard him shout out to Patrick.

"You of course. There's no doubt about it." I heard Patrick reply. Jay awwwed at that and soon enough smooching noises were heard.

I rolled my eyes again which was really ten eye rolling's in one convenient package "Guys I can hear you."

The smooching noise stopped and Jay sounded breathless "Oh sorry. Not my fault there was an irresistible man right here to distract me. Now I was saying that I don't trust this guy."

"You've never even met him." I said paying the driver since the cab had stopped.

"Yeah but everyone knows that blondes are more likely to die more than other hair colors. I mean you alone in an apartment with a guy you don't know is probably the basis for each slasher writer's story. Blondes have more fun and they die first, end of story."

I laughed shaking my head "You do know Patrick is blonde right?"

"Not a natural blonde so he's got immunity. Shit, I gotta go Ry, just be safe ok?"

"Sure." I said walking up the stairs to reach the floor Jason's apartment was on and cutting the call. I wasn't sure what made Jay drop the call so abruptly but I knew that it had something to do with the smooching sounds from earlier.

Rabbits.

Holding the bag with the t-shirt on my left hand, I knocked only twice with my right hand before the door was abruptly opened to reveal a sweaty Jason looking wide eyed behind his glass lens.

"Oh hi." He breathed out smiling.

"Did I catch you at a bad time?" I asked.

"No not really. I was just editing some of the pictures I took today." He explained looking back at his apartment. "It's pretty much what I do almost all the time so no, it's not a bad time I think."

I raised up the hand I held the bag in "Great because I didn't want to hold your shirt captive longer than I should. And trust me it was tempting." I joked.

Jason shook his head "Yeah since I also have your shirt and it would have turned into a weird hostage exchange kind of thing."

I handed it to him giggling "There."

Jason took it and widened his eyes again "Oh shit – I'm so rude letting you stand out in the hallway like this. You should come in."

"Well-" I started since I'd originally planned on handing over the shirt and bolting.

"If you're not busy. I could just hand you your shirt and let you be on your way." Jason rambled off adorably again.

My Algorithms paper was only halfway done and I still had a paper for an elective class pending away for the next week but apart from that I didn't have much going on.

"Ok." I replied.

Jason opened the door to let me in and once again I was greeted by the sight of his well-organized living room and the framed pictures which covered almost all of the walls beautifully. The coffee table was neater than the last time I'd seen it.

The printing paper was stacked right on top of the printer and his laptop was on and showed a picture of the Brooklyn Bridge in a beautiful black and white detail.

"Took a couple of pictures this morning so I'm editing them now." He explained once he saw my eyes wonder towards his computer screen.

"That looks really good." I complimented sitting down on his deep brown couch. Jason blushed a little "Thanks. I try my best at it though. In some ways I feel like I'm pretty mediocre."

"Why do you think that?" I asked interested. He sat on the couch and shrugged "I'm good at most of the basic stuff and a couple of the professional ones but I dropped out of college where I was studying Photography so sometimes I feel like I've missed a lot."

Curious, I asked "Why did you drop out if you don't mind me asking?"

He looked hesitant "This might sound stupid but somehow I felt boxed up? There wasn't as much freedom in expression and creativity as I expected so eventually I felt like it was a waste of time and money so I decided to drop out and start up work anyway. It seemed like a good decision but sometimes I worry that I've made myself lose out on so many stuff."

"Hey, I don't think it's stupid. If you felt like studying Photography at college boxed in your ideas, then it was the right thing to stop it. At the end of the day you're doing all you can to be a good photographer so it doesn't matter if you make through a fancy education or you learn it by your own experience. Besides, our society glorifies drop-outs." I joked making him smile a little.

"I'm pretty sure that only applies to tech geniuses like Bill Gates." He scoffed.

"Maybe they'll make an exception for you." I teased. Jason smile and looked down "Thanks for saying that. It was nice to hear at least one word of encouragement. Most of my family just thinks I'm gambling away my life."

"It's only a gamble if you're not sure what you want or who you want to be." I explained.

Jason glanced at me "I do really. But I wish they could see that."

Normally any emotional talk of any kind made me uncomfortable and eager to leave the premises immediately but Jason had such a warm aura about him that I couldn't help but feel comfortable. He wasn't as confident as most guys but he was great in his own habitat and opened up quite well. We talked about the pictures he'd taken for a little while and he showed me the progress he'd reached on his laptop.

"So you just go out each day and take pictures of the city?" I asked curling my hands on my lap.

Jason laughed "It's not as lifeless as that. I have some paid gigs in the city but this is just part time to build up my portfolio. I'm hoping to get a more permanent job though and maybe an exhibit someday."

"I'm completely sure you will." I replied in confidence. Before he could reply, my phone vibrated in my pocket and I groaned at the interruption. It was Jay calling again.

I didn't know what it was going to be about but I had an idea that it would be long and time consuming so I pocketed my phone once again.

"You know." I said quietly "I have to go now but I don't want to."

He looked surprised about my admission and I was also surprised by myself.

He smiled shyly and dipped his head "If you want, it doesn't have to be the end."

"Huh?" I asked dumbly. Jason picked up his phone from the coffee table "If you haven't deleted my number yet, maybe we could talk later?" Gosh he was so adorable.

"Sure." I said. "I haven't deleted your number yet, I'm not that cruel." I made a mental note to add a smiley face to his contact name later.

"Was really nice to see you again Jason." I smiled a little.

"You too Ryan." He replied rubbing his hand. Then, in a moment I did not see coming, he leaned down and kissed me.........on the cheek.My mouth dropped a little and I could see him smile much wider "Don't want to taint your innocence just yet."

"Ok." I croaked and hurried on my merry little way still feeling the warm kiss throbbing on my cheek. It was only after I'd gone outside that I remembered a single crucial detail.

Of course I forgot to get my shirt back.   -So what do you guys think about Ryan's brother?   -
zoe (after dark)

Chapter 8

----------------------------Hey guys. I was feeling nostalgic for some Ed Sheeran. That explains the song for this chapter. Plus it goes quite well with everything.

SONG - TENERIFE SEA - ED SHEERAN-------------------

"So on scales of one to ten, how nerdy are you?" I asked Jason.

He laughed over the phone "Wow I was kind of waiting for that question to be honest. Maybe like six."

"Six?" I asked leaning over my bathroom counter. "Describe what a stage six nerd entails."

"I like comic books and video games but I draw a line at Star Trek and X Files. That's the side of no return for extreme nerds." He said making me chuckle a little.

His answer made me pout a little even though he couldn't see me over the phone. "That's too sad because I happen to like Star Trek and X-Files.

Almost to borderline obsession.""Oops." He said making me hold in the urge to giggle out. "Then you're an exception. Plus you're cute which gives you obvious immunity."

Compliments were my oxygen day and night since I received so many of them to last me but when Jason called me cute it caused a strange tingling sensation within me. As though it meant so much that he thought of me as cute.

We had been talking none stop since the day I returned his shirt for about a week. It surprised me that I didn't lose interest in him yet like I had originally hoped on. With every conversation we had, I found myself liking him even more than I'd previously anticipated. We had many things in common which evolved past sex and intimacy. For me knowing that I had some sexual chemistry with a guy was good enough, I would work out the rest later.

But with Jason, the necessary things like favorite foods and songs seemed primary.

No one had ever actually cared what my favorite food was before."I just came from shooting at a magazine. Quite exhausting to be honest." He said to me one fine evening. I had finished typing a paper for one of my classes and studied from noon till it was time for dinner.

I had two classes to attend but I ditched them since a nice girl I knew who attended both of them with me promised to email the notes to me.

Most times I found out that skipping a few classes was better because I could still get the gist of it from notes and it gave me time to study more.

"No hot models to warm you up." I teased.

He snorted "Well it was for a home and gardening magazine and I'm not too attracted to cactus and daises so no."

I laughed out at his reply "Oops. Maybe next time."

"I doubt it. Besides I'm not really interested in the models I work with. Feels too much like mixing business with pleasure." I found myself nodding even though he couldn't see. That was quite a stretch to me seeing as pleasure was my business.

"And I don't think any of them would be too eager to date a gay photographer."

And the jackpot was hit.

I'd suspected that Jason wasn't particularly straight and it was hard to sort of deny the subtle tension between us but it was much nicer to hear him actually state that he was gay.

"Too bad for them then." I replied playing with the edge of my sweater.

"If I was a model you'd be the one I'd want shooting me."Silence.

I cringed.

Had I been too forward? Was he even attracted to me? His sexuality didn't guarantee at all that he wanted me even if it did give me a little hope that there was a chance of something happening. But maybe I had been too presumptuous in the first place.

"I bet you'd be quite a sight." His words made me feel warmer. I rubbed the back of my neck with my free hand which wasn't holding a phone. "I wouldn't know. I've never modeled before."

Jason chuckled a little "Doesn't matter. In fact I would be quite flattered to know that I'm the first one."

"Who said that it was going to be you?" I teased.

"Sorry, it was wrong of me to assume.

I envy the person who gets dibs on photographing you for the first time." His voice had gotten huskier, a far cry from the adorable stuttering mess I'd met previously. It might have been because we weren't face to face but he sounded so much more confident when we spoke over the phone.

"So.....do you have any plans this weekend?" Jason asked.

I maneuvered myself around the couch I was sitting on so that I sat up straight "Depends."

"I don't want to sound presumptuous again, but would you like to meet up sometime?" I grabbed one of the couch pillows and squeezed it until my hands turned white. He was asking me out. Jason was asking me out.

"Yes." I replied.

"That sounds great. Maybe Friday night? We could go have dinner or something." He suggested. I bit my lip

"Sure. I'd like that a lot."

"Awesome. Do you particularly have anything you want to do in mind?" He asked.

"Surprise me." I blurted out before I could say something stupid. Of all things I hadn't actually expected him to ask me out on a date. I really didn't see that coming, which was unusual for me.

Normally I could sense from a mile away whenever a guy wanted me. But with Jason I had been too relaxed and easy-going to even focus my energy to care about that.

"I plan to." Jason said softly.

"That sounds great." I said with a smile I couldn't help.

Couldn't wait to tell Jay about this.

"So what does he do for a living?" Jay asked lying down on my bed. I shrugged patting my hair with my hand "He's a photographer."

"Seriously?"

I eyed Jay suspiciously "Yes. Any problem?"

"No it's just that I've never been around to see you date someone who's not an investment banker or lawyer or something." He replied casually.

I frowned "I never actually thought of it like that before."

"That's a good thing though." Jay was quick to say "At least maybe he'll be a lot better than those rich assholes you moan to me about how they have no personality and that their only redeeming qualities are their wallets or penis sizes."

"Jason has a lot of redeeming qualities." I defended.

Jay stretched himself in my bed "That's great. The way I see it he'll definitely be a step-up from all the guys you've been with."

"Why are you talking like it's a sure thing for us to be together? Who knows, maybe he'll piss me off on this first date and I'll kick his artistic little ass to the curb." I said trying for nonchalant as I tried a scarf to see if it matched my jacket.

Jay chuckled "Artistic? Ryan I have never heard you compliment a guy using words other than "handsome" and "not dumb" before. I am really interested in meeting this guy."

When I called him over here to help me find an outfit for my date, I hoped that he wouldn't talk as much. But of course this was Jay and he always had something to say about everything. Spritzing a little Versace Eros on myself, I turned to my best friend in an attempt to change the subject

"Have you solved the mystery behind Patrick's strange behavior yet?"And it worked because Jay sobered up immediately "No. And trust me I've been trying."

"Of course you have." I said with only a hint of sarcasm. He narrowed his eyes at me "He's still been coming home late and smelling like that weird stuff but now he's been taking some money from our joint account without telling me."

My eyes widened, although I wasn't sure which bit of information surprised me more.

The fact that Patrick was actually now taking money without telling his boyfriend with whom he was practically attached at the hip with, or the fact that they were both so disgustingly domestic that they actually had a joint account together.

"There is a reasonable explanation why he must be doing that." I tried to reason.

"Yes. To pay off his meth cooking partners." Jay said stubbornly. There was no reasoning with him now. I tied the laces to my boots. It was a gift from one of my former boyfriend. It was handmade in a little shop in Spain. I'd only worn it twice before.

"Jay why don't you do some more research to actually know if Patrick is doing drugs?" which I doubted he was. Patrick wasn't stupid. He wasn't officially an American citizen yet and obviously wouldn't do anything to damage his chances.

But Jay was delusional and stubborn and I was sure it was partly because he was turned on by the prospect of Patrick being anything other and good and pure. Trust me, I knew him well enough to say that.

He only insisted on the whole meth-cooking theory because he secretly had a thing for bad boy Patrick.Quite twisted.

I was surrounded by too many strange people.

To my surprise, Jason actually took me to the Mexican place I got the taco that he spilled on me. When I asked him why, he replied me "I sort of spoilt your lunch that day and I want to make up for it by taking you here again."

I smiled holding the menu "That's actually really sweet."

"Plus, I'd prefer that whenever I think of tacos, I think of them running down your lips as you try to eat them quickly and not squashed all over your shirt." He said in a soft voice.

I took a small sip of my coke "That sounds like a much better memory in my opinion."

"Speaking of that shirt, it's still in my apartment as we speak." Jason said with an embarrassed laugh. I smiled

"To be honest I kind of forgot about it."

He cocked an eyebrow "You forgot about your five hundred dollar shirt? That seems like an awful lot of money to just forget."

I shrugged not wanting to say that I had shoes which were more expensive than that.

Suddenly I felt embarrassed that I actually did have stuff like that. "I like you like this."

"How?" Jason asked.

"Confident. Not so shy. Like you were really cute when you rambled and all but I like this more......confident you better." I said hoping not to offend him.

He blinked then smiled a little "Ah, yeah. Sorry but I just get quite nervous around you, well I did. Now that we've been talking I feel at ease now."

"Why were you shy?" I tilted my head to the side.

The waiter came with the food we had ordered previously and set it down before he continued. "Well it's not every day that you bump into a hot guy in the most embarrassing way ever." Then he chuckled in a self-depreciating way.

"You looked so.....hot and you were so mad at the same time and I didn't know what to do with myself. So I just kept stuttering and blushing like an idiot." He said blushing as he spoke.

His honesty and openness warmed me like never before. I was so used to seeing the men around me hide who they really were and maintain facades to impress or remain in control.

Jason didn't try to be any of those things. He actually wasn't afraid to let me know how he felt the first time we met and I appreciated that.

"If it's any consolation, I was caught between remaining mad or cooing at how cute you were." I teased a little. Jason grinned "Now I feel less stupid."

We talked a little, mostly adding up on the stuff we'd spoken about before during the week. I bit into my delicious enchiladas humming at his every reply. I enjoyed talking to Jason. The only people I'd enjoyed talking to were Jay, Patrick and parents. And the only other friend I'd ever made in my life.

"So are you originally from New York?"

I shook my head "No. From Greendale in Massachusetts."

"Cool, I'm from DC." Jason replied.

"Why did you move down here?"

I shrugged "Why did you move down here?"

"Opportunities. New York has more opportunities in terms of jobs and the entertainment industry over here."

He replied dipping a celery stick into sour yogurt "You haven't answered me."

"College." I replied hastily shoving a nacho into my mouth. "I liked the program here better. Plus I needed to get away from Greendale."

"Why?" He asked and I realized that I'd said too much.

I chewed thoughtfully "The town I grew up in was quite……toxic. It wasn't a blast living there and I was so excited when I got out. You'll know all my reasons when I'm ready to tell."

"Of course." He said so understandingly "I won't push it."

But when would I really be ready to tell him? That I'd had so many issues and problems I couldn't help but forget? Was I actually going to tell him that he was relatively the most normal person I'd been with?

"Is something wrong?"

I was immediately snapped out of my thought train "Of course not. Just in a little daze is all." Jason looked quite concerned but he let me be.

After dinner, we both split the check since neither of us could decide who to pay. He held my hand as we walked out of the restaurant "I really liked that."

"Me too." I mumbled clumsily a little giddy from the warmth of his hand on mine. It was a starry night which was quite unusual and it was the first time I actually felt nervous about impressing a date.

Mostly it was about what they did to impress me so that I didn't get bored but I liked how Jason's eyes seemed to hold a little glint when he looked at me.

"And if it isn't too much trouble, I'd like to see you again." He said unsure of himself as though he didn't know if I would say no or not. I nodded "I'd also like that a lot."

Then, in an unexpected move, he leaned forward and pressed his lips gently on mine. It was a careful sort of kiss, as if he was just testing the waters. I deepened it and placed my hand at the back of his head to assure him that yes I wanted this.

He tasted like the spicy Buffalo wings we'd had earlier but I savored it anyway just because it was Jason.

His left hand moved to my waist and pushed me towards his chest and I absolutely melted like a teenager at the action.

We pulled away not too long after that "That was nice."

"Yeah." He replied shyly. Jason kissed my forehead "Want me to take a cab with you home?"

I shook my head "Your place is closer. I'll be fine."

"Ok." He said kissing me briefly again before turning to hail me a cab like a true gentleman. Sitting in the taxi and still very conscious of my swollen lips, I realized then how truly fucked I now was.

I sorta ship them. What about you guys?

And who's heard The 1975's new album?

Chapter 9

-----------------------I really enjoyed writing this chapter a lot. Like more than usual. Like a lot.

SONG - LOVE ON THE BRAIN - RIHANNA-----------------------

I hated cooking.

Ok maybe that was a slight exaggeration. Cooking wasn't my favorite thing was a much better thing to say. In fact, if it wasn't for the constant threat of cholesterol clogging my arteries from too much greasy takeout food, the fact that I needed to keep my figure and remain that I didn't always trust already made salads from Whole Foods, I probably would have eaten takeout all the days of my life.

But sadly health was a priority. And I didn't want my shiny granite kitchen to go to waste, so I'd made a rule that I cooked at least twice a week and no more than that. And since I mostly thrived on salads and nuts, it was no real problem. The only down turn was that I had a very limited knowledge of recipes which I never actually considered a real problem before.

Well, that was until I'd invited Jason for dinner at my apartment and had no idea what to cook.

Then my ignorance had become a real problem.

The funny thing about it all was that during the actual conversation, I was confident and sure of myself. Jason said that he'd had more gigs than he'd anticipated during the week so he barely ate anything other than hotdogs and subs. And I, being in trying to be caring, blurted out that I could make him dinner on Saturday as a treat for all the hard work he'd done. Specifically, beef stroganoff and crab salad which he'd mentioned was his favorite.

Jason's breathy thanks and compliments made me smile until I dropped the call and realized that I had absolutely no idea how to cook any of the dishes he'd mentioned. After a panicked call to Jay who laughed at me for a painfully long time, I searched the internet for any decent recipes.

"Should I just ask for your apartment number at the lobby?" Jason asked on the phone as I stirred the spices into the sour cream.

"Yeah, the guy in front will direct you right to my apartment." I replied tapping the stirring spoon on the rim of the pot.

I couldn't help the nervous feeling in my chest as I anticipated his arrival. It was because I missed him and wanted our second date to go well, but mostly because I'd never cooked for anyone before and didn't want my first time to go wrong at all. Jay would definitely laugh his ass off if I ended up killing my date.

Sooner than I'd expected, there was a soft knock on my door. Throwing the tea towel into the sink, I ran to the front door to unlock it while nervously patting my clothes on the way. I opened the door to see Jason's soft smile waiting for me.

"Hey." He said.

"Hi." I replied moving forward to place a light kiss on his lips. Taking the initiative, he deepened it placing his hand on the nape of my neck to pull me closer. Something inside of me coiled intensely and I let out a small moan before finally pulling away.

He cradled my cheek "I've kind of been thinking about that for a while. Sorry."

"I was the one who attacked you in the first place." I said with a cheeky smile. He laughed "It's ok. Good thing I really don't mind."

I pecked his lips again "We should probably go before the food gets cold."

"Good idea." He said following me into the apartment. I walked into the living room "Feel free to sit anywhere you like." My L shaped couched was quite spacious which was where he sat while I went to the kitchen to get our food.

"Nice place."

"Thanks." I said dishing our food into two separate plates. I knew that the next thought on his mind was how a college student could afford such pricey place. During our conversations, I was mostly vague about my answers. I couldn't actually tell him that I'd practically made a career out of dating men who could buy me whatever I wanted. What was I actually doing? What was I doing with a guy who I didn't even know how to answer? How was I going to explain myself to him?

My hands trembled slightly as I served the food into our plates.

"No offense, but how do you afford this place? It's really really nice." Jason said with his curiosity obviously peaking up.

"Um, it's a funny story actually." I started trying to think fast of a lie "My grandma actually left a lot of money before she died. Half of it went towards my college fund while I used the rest to buy a place here since I'd always wanted to move to New York."

Both of my grandmas were dead. One died before I was born while the other died when I was six years old.

And they didn't leave anything but moth-ball infested trunks of nothing. I hoped that Jason would believe me story.

"She must have loved you an awful lot." Jason said with a signature smile. "Did you design it yourself?"

I nodded frantically feeling the relief wash right off me like a wave that he actually ate up my story "I've got a keen eye for interior design." The boyfriend who'd bought my apartment was a visiting English Lord who'd been so infatuated with me that he gave me money to buy any apartment I wanted and dubbed it "our place" after we'd only been dating for three weeks.

A few weeks later, he wife came with an ultimatum to ruin him that if he divorced her for a man and disgraced their name in the papers, she would walk away with all of his money and ruin his title.

His choice was a no-brainer. There were people much shallower than me in the world.

"You really do. It's got a nice subtle class about it." Jason admired.

I smiled at him from the kitchen hoping that he would really stop talking about my house. "Wanna eat on the dining table or couch?"

"Couch is fine."

"Alright then." I said bringing our steaming plates and placing them on the coffee table. I also brought some water and a moderately priced bottle of wine because I didn't want to bring any cause for questioning.

"Ohhh fancy." He teased eyeing the bottle of wine.

I shrugged "Got a little raise at work so I decided, why not?"

Jason immediately looked somber "You didn't have to if it cost a lot." He sounded o considerate as though it actually made him feel upset that I had to spend money. I shook my head "It's ok. Really wasn't expensive at all, plus I just wanted to have something nice to go with our dinner."

He smiled again and kissed my forehead "That's awesome. But next time I'll buy the wine."

Next time.

He was actually considering a next time.

"That's great and all but could you please taste your food now? I wanna know if it's perfect." I pleaded nervously. He grinned nodding his head "Sure." Then took a forkful to his mouth chewing it carefully. My chest clawed from the inside out trying to figure out if he thought it was good or not.

Jason swallowed "That was really good."

My eyes brightened "Really? You're not just saying that?"

He grinned "Sweetheart I don't just say things. I actually think it's really delicious."

"So I'm not going to have to awkwardly explain to a doctor that I wasn't trying to poison you or something?"

He laughed wiping his mouth a serviette I'd dropped on the coffee table "Not at all. You're a pro at this."

I blushed "Actually I've never made this till today."

Jason froze in the middle of putting the fork in his mouth "Seriously? But this is so good. You must have a gift."

I laughed keeling from all the praise I was receiving "I just followed the recipe to be honest."

Jason had this strangle twinkle in his eye "Then interior design is not your only talent then." I poured the wine into two glasses and handed him one "Then hopefully I'll be able to explore any other talents I have hiding inside."

"Maybe." He said still eyeing me as he carefully took a sip. There was just something about this version of Jason that made me feel.....well good. He was confident and not as shy as before and quite flirty to be honest but he maintained an impressive boundary. He was self-assured but it wasn't in the over pompous manner I'd seen several times before in the men before him. He didn't act as though I needed to kneel before him. He just acted like a guy who knew exactly what he was good for and wasn't going to back away.

All through dinner we chatted about any topic that came up. He told me about his family and life in DC, about his father had died quite early in his life and his mother took it hard. He said that it was painful but it made them grow closer together. Jason also told me some funny stories about his dad's brother and wife who lived just down the street from them and always snooped around in he and his mother's business but with good intentions.

"Sometimes we didn't even need to have lunch or dinner because my Aunt always made enough for the whole street." He said with a smile recalling the memory. "In fact we barely cooked anything in my house because there was no need to. Aunt Vera always had plenty of food for everyone, even when my friends would show up for dinner sometimes."

"Sounds like you enjoyed it a lot." I said.

"Yeah I did. Was nice to be around family, everyone was so warm and the food was always great." He reminisced.

During my own teen years, dinner was a mostly awkward affair because I had a brother who could barely look at me most of the time due to the fact that he despised me for being who I was. My parents always tried to intervene but Chris was always so stubborn. After a while I'd grown just as stubborn and refused to beg for the attention of someone who could barely acknowledge me.

"Was just plain ole boring in my house." I said sipping my wine. "And I didn't really have friends over."

Jason seemed surprised by my confession "Really? I totally saw you as the type who had a constant horde of friends around you."

I laughed bitterly "Quite the opposite. Nobody really wanted to be friends with the nerdy gay kid." Who was also a little chubby but I didn't add that part. It wasn't until my senior year that people began vying for my attention, even though it was pretty much the wrong kind of attention.

Jason looked concerned at what I'd said "Were you bullied Ryan?"

His voice was so quiet and understanding that I honestly couldn't take it. He sounded like.....he actually cared if I got bullied before. As if the very thought upset him in some way.

I shook my head "Just standard name-calling and being ignored most of the time. Nothing big." I toned it down for him because I wasn't ready to reveal the horrors of my high school life to him just yet. Jason shifted closer to me and hugged my shoulder "Just because it wasn't big doesn't mean that it wasn't wrong. Everyone is so ignorant in high school, which is ironic seeing as they're in school to learn."

I laughed at that "Yeah but even adults have their own degree of ignorance."

"I just hate the fact that you weren't happy at some point in your life." He said in a much softer tone. "If I'd known you then, I'd probably be making up ways to be your friend."

I snorted because I didn't see it as true but decided not to argue. I liked how Jason made me feel. A part of me was perturbed about how perfect he was while the other half decided to enjoy it as much as I could.

"I doubt that, but thanks." I said in gratitude. We had shifted much closer so much that it almost seemed as though we were cuddling but I didn't mind and neither did Jason. His hazel eyes seemed so much better up close and I kept feeling the urge to bury my face in the crook of his neck because of how warm I thought it would feel. How safe it would feel.

And it scared me.

I only cuddled in the past out of duty and felt happy at the men who didn't like contact after sex. We hadn't even had sex yet and I wanted to have Jason's arms around me so badly.

My head was bursting in contradictions.

His thumb brushed the top of my lip and I noticed how intently he had been staring at my lips. I teased him by flicking the tip of my tongue on his thumb "Son of a bitch." He swore breathlessly.

"You can kiss me you know." I whispered because there was no need to talk loudly with our proximity. He hummed then gently kissed me. I placed my hands around his neck immediately while he put his hands around my waist pressing our chests together. I slid my tongue across his lips taking in their soft velvety feel and moaned when he did the same to mine. One of his hands moved up to the nape of my neck again as our tongues danced further together.

Without realizing it, my hands had begun gently unbuttoning Jason's plaid shirt as he traced kisses down the hollow of my neck until his chest was finally free of fabric. It nearly killed me to feel his hard chest as I rubbed my hands up and down taking in this fine species of man.

"Take it off please." I said into the outer shell of his ear before biting his earlobe. Jason groaned quickly removing the offending piece of fabric and helping me take mine off.

"You're gorgeous." I said.

He pressed a kiss unto my bare shoulder "Ditto babe."

I stood up quickly which caused Jason to give me a confused look but relaxed when he saw that I was taking off my jeans and boxers. His watchful gaze never left me as I stood naked not feeling a shred of vulnerability before slowly getting on my knees to unzip his jeans. His eye immediately went dark at the realization of what I was about to do came crashing.

With a wicked smile, I pulled out his impressive cock and flicked the tip with my tongue make shock waves go through Jason.

"Ohh." He moaned throwing his head back. "That's mean babe."

"Mean is my middle name." I said before taking his whole dick into my mouth. It amazed me how beautiful he looked grabbing one of the couch pillows and groaning curses out at my skillful tongue. I closed my eyes and hummed, throwing myself completely into the task of pleasuring Jason. His pleasure was my pleasure.

"How do you feel?" I asked deliberately making my hot breath fan all over his penis.

"Amazing." He choked out much to my pleasure.

"Good." I purred standing up. I reached under the couch to bring out the condom and lube I'd hid in anticipation of Jason's visit.

"You were expecting this weren't you?" He asked widening his legs. I tore off the condom with my teeth "Maybe. Maybe I'd been thinking about it ever since I invited you for dinner."

"Oh really?" He grinned as I pulled off his jeans and boxers. I carefully rolled the condom over his dick and gave it light kiss before uncapping the lube. I moaned as I forced two fingers into my hole. It felt so good but what I really needed was Jason's cock inside me urgently. I placed a third finger after about two minutes then turned to face him "So much. I've wanted to fuck you for so long. So fucking long."

I continued to finger myself when I felt another hand on mine pulling my fingers out and replacing them.

Then a sensual voice in my ear "Let me do it."

I nearly cried riding his thick fingers almost to completion, but the main prize was his dick and that was what I was going to have. I bucked my hips on his fingers before turning to engage him in a messy kiss. I ran my fingers through his hair pulling with every desperate buck.

"Please. Jason I need you." I begged like the whore I was.

"Of course." He murmured taking out his fingers and gently guiding my hips over his hard rock dick. I sunk gently, making a strange noise in between crying and gasping and sat completely on his lap. We were still for a moment. No movement. Our common sense had been replaced by a glorious haze of lusty passion and wasn't clearing up at all.

Then, Jason held my hips firmly pulling himself out gently until only the tip was left which made me whine terribly, before thrusting back in causing my face to form an O expression.

Then he began thrusting into me like a wild animal.

"Fuck!" I shouted grabbing unto his back hard as though I was afraid he would leave without me. My mouth could hardly close because I shouted all sorts of words I didn't even know, screaming at the sensation he'd stirred in me. When he hit my bundle of nerves I completely lost it.

"Jason!" I screamed digging my nails so hard into his back I was sure it drew blood.

"Oh say my name again." He demanded.

"Jason." I moaned out repeating it over and over again. "Please."

"Please what babe?" He grunted holding my hips like they were a lifeline. What was it I wanted? Harder? Faster? Deeper? I didn't know exactly what it was. All I knew that I wanted was-

"More."

And he gave it right to me. I was seeing not even stars, but strokes of galaxies passing me over and over again. The intense look on Jason's face as he was about to climax made me shot ropes of cum all over his chest without warning. And my mine must have triggered his because he came shortly after gripping my hips and burying his face in my neck with a loud groan of pleasure.

Tired, we both laid on my couch much too word out to bother moving to my bedroom. My head was one his chest while his hand stroked my back occasionally.

"Wow." Jason said after a while.

"Wow is right." I said with a smug smile that he kissed right off my face.

Maybe cooking wasn't so bad after all.

.........So that happened..........

Happy Women's Day btw. Nothing more lovely than being strong and female.

Chapter 10 (Greendale)

-----------------Gotten into the habit of making banners. If any of you would like to make banners for this story, you can PM me :)

Anyways, remember that all chapters with Greendale mean that we're in the timeline when Ryan was a teenager and still living in his hometown. Just a refresher.

SONG - DEVIL SIDE - FOXES ---------------------

I had been back to school a whole month and I still couldn't get over the way people stared at me in school. It was quite fascinating at first, and then it became predictable. Walking to my locker, the classrooms, the gym, the cafeteria, it was all the same whenever people spotted me. Their thoughts had become so obvious the might as well have been dangling over their heard in white little bubbles.

"Omg, how did Ryan Perry get so hot?" "Was it surgery? It totally must have been surgery for him to look like that not. But do guys, like, do plastic surgery?" "Damn he should totally tell me how he lost that weight."

I didn't have plastic surgery.

Not even close.

It was funny how people nowadays now assumed that the only way to lose some mild waste was surgery.

Nathan Coffey and his friends didn't come near me which both surprised and didn't surprise me. I somehow expected them not to let me off so easily even if it was to taunt me about how nothing had changed. But no taunts came. I noticed Nathan eyeing me a few times but brushed it off and enjoyed my newfound freedom and confidence. When people now stared at me, it wasn't out of pity but out of awe and even jealously. Want had also become a common factor towards me.

Girls flirted with me dropping me small gifts and tokens. The guys who were bold enough flirted from afar since they didn't want their girlfriends to find out.

Some of it was maybe wrong, but I was enjoying it too much to care. For once I had the power and I was going to take full advantage of it. And when my opportunity came to do so, it was very unexpected.

It was a particularly slow day. Shelley Baker had been trying to hang off me during Art class and I escaped to the boy's locker room to get away from her. I also needed to change my shirt since I'd spilled paint on it in Art class and didn't want to walk around covered in paint. My spare clothes were in my gym bag in case of emergencies.

When I got there, I didn't think to find out if I was the only one and went straight to my locker. I changed and was in the middle of stuffing my paint covered t-shirt into my gym bag when I got startled.

"Hey."

My heart nearly jumped out of my chest when I turned to see Emmett Anderson, Nathan's best friend. He just stood there with his towel tied around his waist and wet hair dripping unto the tiles, watching me intently.

"What do you want?" I asked nervously.

Maybe I'd been too confident to think that Nathan would leave me alone just because I looked different. He'd always had it out for me not matter what and it seemed like that fact would never change.

But Emmett only smiled slyly "You should know what I want."

"I'm not a mind-reader dude." I said with a nervous smile of my own.

He walked closer and put his hand on my side, causing my insides to freeze like I was doused with cold water. His callused thumb brushed against my bare skin and his face became closer to mine "I want you. Now."

What?

Did Emmett Anderson just admit that he wanted me?

In what seemed to be a more than platonic manner?

"I've wanted you for such a long time now." He confessed shocking me even more. "But Nathan hated you all this time and you were so......not as attractive as you are now." Of course he would say something like that. "But now you are and even if Nathan doesn't still like you, he can't do anything about it now because everyone will think he's jealous or something."

Emmett had just sold his best friend down the river because of one lusty moment. A slow smile crept unto my face "Well I've liked you for a while too."

"Really?" Emmett's face brightened even more.

The truth was that I had never really paid particular attention to Emmett in the past. He was the best friend of my oppressor and I really didn't see anything tying us together. He was on the football team and part of the people I didn't like because of how they treated me. Emmett never particularly shoved or hit me the way Nathan did, but laughing and taunting was just a cruel. He'd come up with one of my most popular nicknames, fat fag, after he and Nathan found a couple of gay porn magazines in my bag pack that I'd accidentally brought to school and then outed me before my time.

This was the same guy who confessed that he'd had a thing for me even before the summer. A sinister voice at the back of my head told me that I could use him to my advantage. Emmett seemed like the kind of idiot to out his friend for a good fuck. And I wouldn't mind having some dirt on Nathan Coffey at all.

"Yes. That's why I went away this summer." I said throwing my hands around his shoulder. "So that I could do everything possible to be good enough for you."

"Well you are now." He said making my stomach twist with disdain. The asshole.

But I kept it up "Yes. Now I'll be all yours Emmy."

He seemed to like my stupid nickname because his dick hardened almost immediately and brushed against my thigh.

"We can't still be seen together." He warned quickly. "I have a reputation and no one can know that I like...guys. I'm not gay though."

Predictable as ever denying his already obvious sexuality. "Of course. It'll just be between you and me."

Emmett grinned and roughly kissed me. It was messy and not particularly enjoyable because of all the teeth and tongue rolled in at the same time unskillfully, but I made all the right sounds to let him think he was the best kisser on earth.

That was when I'd turned into someone else. My transformation wasn't even when I'd gone away for a total makeover during the summer, but at that moment when Emmett expressed his attraction towards me. That was when it really occurred to me that I was wanted, lusted even. I could make anyone give me anything or do anything I wanted just because of my looks. It was a feeling I'd never experienced before and it was fucking euphoric at the moment.

And like what I'd been taught, I was going to use it right to my advantage.

I'd never actually hooked up with Emmett until three weeks later. By then he was so into me that he'd have jumped over a cliff if it meant I would do a striptease for him. When we were at a club in the next town over, Emmett accidentally revealed to me that Nathan had an older brother after a few too many beers.

He said that he was the Coffey's pride and joy and that Nathan looked up to him so much. Emmett also said that the guy was pretty private and hadn't been seen with too many girls and was quite touchy on the subject.

That was when a plan began racing in my mind.

I was going to meet this Gerald Coffey and fuck him to ruin his brother.

This was short but it needed to be.

Chapter 11

--

---------------------Banners anyone......ok next time then.

SONG - VOLCANO - THE VAMPS

"Good morning." I nearly dropped the spatula I was holding when the back of my neck was attacked by a pair of warm lips. I smiled "Won't be a very good one if I end up ruining our breakfast will it?"

Jason hummed "Doesn't matter to me as long as I've got you here in my arms." Then his arms wrapped around my torso, intensifying my smile.

"As nice as that is, I can't eat your arms." I said playfully.

He laughed pressing one more kiss to my neck before pulling away to face me properly "I was a little sad when I woke up and didn't find you beside me. Thought you'd gone, until I realized that this was your apartment."

I laughed "I wouldn't have gone either way. Just needed to refresh us with some sustenance."

Jason kissed my neck again murmuring, "You're all the sustenance I need." The whole situation was so ridiculously sweet but I couldn't bring myself to care for one moment. I completely indulged myself in the sweetness, who cared if I had a rotten tooth later?

I whisked the batter a little more before pouring it into the frying pan, "But just to be on the safe side, we should totally have some pancakes."

"Mmm, these smell good." He commented moving away from my body to stand beside me, "I have high hopes for how good they're going to be."

"Thought I proved how great my cooking was last night." I said pretending to sound hurt.

"Oh no you did, I just like being surprised when you keep proving it over again." He replied with a wink. I smiled, flipping the pancake over, "Good choice of words. Now go sit so I can serve your breakfast."

He mock saluted me "Yes sir."

I rolled my eyes but smiled anyway.

Jason and I enjoyed a pleasant breakfast before he had to go back to his own apartment to get ready for a shoot he was doing in Midtown. For some ridiculous reason, his absence made me feel down but I texted him and brushed the feeling right off. Just because we'd had two dates and spent the night together after sex didn't mean that we needed to form some sort of ridiculous co-dependency. I was my own person and I wouldn't stop being my own person just because I was now with Jason.

Your own person would be scouting the next deep pocketed guy to catch, a distant thought slithered from the depths of my brain.

I shook my head trying to get it off. I didn't mean that particular part of me. Jason and I had started on a good note and I intended for it to remain that way. He was nice, sweet and humble, brilliant refreshment from dating stuffy, self-centered men. Besides I had a fine sum tucked away in my savings account.

I was content.

For now, the same nasty thought repeated.

I dropped my mug of coffee into the sink going off to shower. Hopefully the warm water would be enough to clear my thoughts.

It was a particularly slow day. My classes dragged on much to my irritation and Jason had a very hectic photo shoot from what he'd managed to tell me which meant his texts were scarce so I couldn't even enjoy the pleasure of talking to him.

The professor in my last class droned on about an assignment we were supposed to hand in. I'd already started it and was halfway through, so I pretty much ignored the information. On the way out of the lecture hall, my phone vibrated and I fished it out to answer. The caller ID stated that it was my Dad. I had mixed feelings.

"Hi Dad."

"Hey kid." His voice was soft and raspy like I'd always remembered. If there was anything that made me homesick at all, it would be my father's voice and my mother's pies. Just those two things. They'd always brought me comfort through my tearful High School years.

"Some fire finally burn Greendale or what?" I joked.

My Dad scoffed "Not at all. What makes you think I only call you to talk about gossip?"

"I dunno Dad. Maybe past experience?" I said sarcastically making him laugh on the other end.

My Dad and I had the sort of relationship most parents would wish to have with their kids. We were close, peas in a pod. I'd been his favorite child despite all. When I came out of the closet to my family, my mother cried and wailed and didn't talk to me until the next day when she revealed that she loved me and only reacted that way because she was scared and confused by my confession. My mother had always been a black and white person who only saw things in two dimensions. My sexuality had crossed quite a grey line in her mind but she accepted me all the same.

Whereas my dad stood up from his chair and nearly bone crushed me with a hug, saying that he loved me even if I brought a donkey home. Simple and without hesitation. I remember fighting the happy tears in my eyes when I assured him that I wasn't going to be bringing home any donkeys.

Chris had just stood there unmoved as if I hadn't said a damn thing. Then I'd assumed that he just didn't know what to say and would come around later. It was later that night that we'd bumped into each other on my way to the bathroom that he'd called me a stupid fag that I realized he wasn't going to come around to anything. My brother was in a white and black dilemma of his own. He'd already had it bad being the brother of a bullied nerd, being the brother of a gay bullied nerd would surely be the end of him.

At least that's how I expected Chris felt.

"Well sadly I've got no gossip but I just wanted to know how you were doing." He said softly.

I shrugged "Thanks Dad. I'm doing great actually."

"Sure? Because you sound as great as a deflated tired."

I bit my lip to hold in my laughter "I'm great Dad. School's going well and I'm as boring as ever."

"I see. Not dating anyone?"

"Dad." I groaned out running my hand through my hair "Please don't ask me that yet."

"Why not?" He almost whined. "Chris and your Mom talk about his girlfriend's all the time and I feel left out."

My body tensed a little at the mentioned of my brother but I giggled anyway "And so you wanted to talk about my boyfriends with me?"

"Plural form, that's a good sign." Dad teased. I shook my head even though he couldn't see me "No not really."

"Why? You never seem to date and I'm worried for you son." If only he knew. "Besides with the number of parades happening these days you might as well just drop into one of them and find yourself a husband."

"Dad!" one disadvantage of having a close relationship with parents is that they maintain full rights to embarrass you at will. I was glad my Dad was quite accepting about my sexuality, but his insistence on me finding a husband was borderline ridiculous now.

"Don't Dad me now. There's nothing wrong in making sure my son doesn't remain lonely for the rest of his life." My parents had an idea of the scandal I caused in my high school leaving Greendale. Not everyone knew and those who did certainly didn't tell to remain their images. I'd told my Dad who didn't bat an eyelash when I wanted to leave and never come back. He paid for my ticket to New York and bid me a good time in college. I had a scholarship and some money saved up so I didn't have anything really keeping me back.

I told my Dad everything but about my life and relationships in New York. He didn't know that I dated for money, or the many men I'd slept with just to maintain the kind of the life I was already used to. I knew he would always understand, but I didn't still want to risk disappointing him.

Moving to this city had made me shameless about what I did. But somehow I was afraid that revealing it to my Dad would bring back the conscience I'd long thrown away.

"I'll be fine Dad. I am fine." I assured him.

"I just want you to happy Ryan. I know you've proved that you can do the whole independence thing wonderfully and that you don't need someone to be happy but I don't want you to be lonely at the same time." He said in his all-knowing fatherly wisdom.

I bit my lip again "I might be seeing someone."

"What's his name?" Dad asked in a sing-song excited way. I rolled my eyes but smiled at his antics "His name is Jason and he's wonderful. But don't keep your fingers crossed because we're just starting out and seeing where all of this goes."

"Hey just knowing is enough for me. Does he treat you right?" He demanded all protective.

I laughed "Dad, he is! He's great but we're still seeing how this goes."

"That's amazing Ryan. You deserve all the happiness in the world." He said happily.

"Thanks Dad." I replied quietly. "I love you."

"And I love you too." The line went dead.

The mixed feelings I always had talking to my Dad were happiness and guilt. Happiness because he was my favorite person ever and talking to him always brought a smile to my face, guilt because I was keeping parts of my life secret from him. He told me everything and yet I couldn't return the same courtesy because I was afraid of what he would think about me. That was one of the cons of it; I couldn't tell my Dad about my relationships because I didn't want to give anything away.

I went home after my classes and tried to call Jason but I couldn't get him at all which meant he was still doing his photo shoot.

Instead of studying, I opened a bottle of wine and wrapped myself in an afghan on the couch. My body didn't want to do anything but relax until I got to talk to Jason. Briefly, I wondered if my Dad would like Jason. They both had the same taste in football teams and food. My Dad would probably dish up stories about my time as a kid, watching Jason as he tried not to laugh but would fail miserably. Dad would probably awe at Jason's pictures and not even bat an eyelash as his lack of a college degree. Jason would eagerly eat up the boring details of Dad's architectural business and maintain an actual interest in all his ventures.

It made my heart yearn to think that such a future was possible.

I berated myself mentally for having such thoughts.

I was the one who insisted on keeping things slow, yet here I was daydreaming about a white picket fence already.

There was a loud knock on my door which made me frown. It couldn't have been Jason since he'd definitely call and let me know if he was coming just to be polite. I wasn't expecting any visitors and Jay didn't say anything about coming over today.

Against my better judgment, I opened the door to reveal a haggard Brian. His usually pretentious gelled hair was wild and sticking out in different directions. His suit was straight but his tie was loosened with the top button undone. He had a wild look in his eye.

"Ryan, babe I missed you so much-"

"What are you doing here?" I said stepping back.

"I missed you ok? I haven't had a decent fuck in so long and I miss you're smoking body so much." He said moving closer but I stopped him with a hand to the chest.

"In case you forgot, we're broken up. Which means you should find an alternative means to wet your dick." I said calmly.

Brian sighed in frustration "Please Ryan I'm begging you. I'll buy you whatever the fuck you want, a car, a townhouse, a fucking rocket to the moon. I won't be a jealous bastard anymore."

I folded my hands amused "Sorry. Answer is still no. Besides I have a boyfriend now." His desperation the turned into anger. "So that's it? You're going to toss me aside because you now have a new piggy bank to play with?"

"Brian leave." I said with thinning patience. "What I do isn't your business."

"How much does he pay you huh? A million a night to play with your ass?" He said sounding more crazed each second. It scared me a little to think that a lack of sex could turn someone into this.

"You're disturbing my neighbors. I'm calling security." I pushed the door but he didn't budge.

"Please, I'm fucking miserable. I haven't had sex in so long and my fucking fiancée won't even give me a simple blowjob. All she wants is stupid missionary." Brian begged. My mouth couldn't help but widened at the sight of tears glistening in his eyes. He was really that desperate.

"Get a Grindr account, it'll save you money." I saidfinally slamming the door in his face causing him to scream from the other side.Then I called Pete downstairs to take Brian's name off my visitors list forgood.

Ryan had some really deep thoughts back there. Who else thinks so?

And I've entered this story into the Grand LGBT Awards, so you guys should vote it you want this story to win!

New Name

H ey guys. I hate author's notes but this needs to be said. I'm changing this stories name from Call Me Easy to Wayward because I think it fits the story more and sounds a bit mature.

Just letting y'all know to avoid confusion.

I will delete this authors note after a while.

Chapter 12

- -

- - - - - - - - - - - - - - -

SONG - WET THE BED - CHRIS BROWN

A little smut because you deserve it.

- - - - - - - - - - - - - - - - - - -

"I honestly think that this is a little pretentious." I said in all seriousness at the movie we were watching. Jason looked amused "Really? What's so pretentious about an art film?"

I turned to face him from where my head was on his lap "Are you really asking what's pretentious about an art film?" I said. "The fact that's it's called an art film is pretentious. It's literally got no clear plot but it'll win awards at Cannes and critics will call it amazing anyway because it's supposed to have some vague lesson about love."

Jason laughed "You're really opinionated you know that?" I was currently spending the night at Jason's apartment. Normally we alternated between both our places for the past two months we'd been dating but I'd been at his for the past three days since we'd had most of our dates within the area.

He'd convinced me to watch some French art film but all I seemed to do was criticize it. It was a fairly nice day; the weather was actually in our favor for one of the few times I'd lived in this city but staying inside to watch a movie instead of having dinner out seemed so much more appealing.

"Really? They meet but she won't take her back? Oh what she so she sticks with the person she's unhappy with because she thinks it's the right thing? Of course there's a fireworks scene." I rambled on until the credits began rolling.

"Well at least I learned a valuable lesson tonight." Jason said facing me.

"That it was all really pretentious?" I asked in victory thinking he'd seen my point.

"That you don't appreciate good prose." He said with a laugh. I glared at him moving up to straddle his waist so that we were face to face "That was not prose. We just watched a movie about two girls who fall in love in at a duck pond after yelling at each other for no good reason. I think you need to be educated on what a good movie is."

"Really?" he raised an eyebrow.

"Yes and I'll be sure to educate you in the fine works of cinematography but right now." I moved my waist in a slow figure eight earning a hiss from Jason, "You seem to want something else taken care of."

"I honestly had no idea this would lead to sex." He said breathlessly rubbing his lips on my neck, causing several goose bumps to appear. "If I didn't know any better, I'd say those lesbians seemed to have turned you on."

I grinned widening my legs to accommodate him "I'll assure you now that what's under me right now is that turned me on. Not those." The suggestion made me shiver a little. I didn't understand how they could do it, but I can't survive without dick.

"Do you want to be on top?" Jason asked tentatively.

I'd topped only once since we'd been together but Jason seemed to enjoy it well enough. As much as I liked being the top, there was something much more intimate and a little sexier about being on the bottom. It was mostly about being held close, looking into his eyes with each and every thrust he gave.

"I want you inside me now." I whispered against his lips. My words must have had quite an effect because he roughly thrusted against me and his erection was now diamond mast hard. His eyes were hooded and I noticed how much lust was slowly overtaking.

"We should go to my room." He said in a tone that reflected his thinning patience. Gracefully, I slid off his lap and walked to the bedroom I'd become quite acquainted with in the past few months, walking slowly to torture him even more like the wicked being I was. I threw myself on his comfortable queen sized bed and closed my eyes.

I didn't even open them when I heard the door close or when I heard the clattering of a belt on the floor. Not even when I felt his cold hands going under my shirt and I shivered a little in delight. Not even when he moved on top of me, positioning his knees on either side to anchor his body above mine. Jason brushed his lips against my neck. His favorite part of my body, he once admitted.

"You're lovely."

I opened my eyes.

He was staring right at me. It should have creeped me out or made me shake off our intense eye contact but I couldn't help but stare right back.

"So are you." I replied sincerely.

He smiled in that little self-depreciating way I'd always hated. He had no right to think he wasn't handsome or hot enough. I'd gone through the battle enough in my life but I wasn't going to let an actual perfect human being feel that way.

I cradled his face in my palm "You're so lovely. I could spend all night looking at you and still marvel at it. This isn't a fib to get into your pants; it's the real truth and nothing but." I didn't add that sometimes I had a problem understanding what the truth was really and what it wasn't.

Jason smiled kissing my palm "I'd still let you get into my pants either way."

That got us both chuckling.

"Wait." He said when I attempted to remove his shirt for him. Noting my confusion, he quickly added "I want to try something with you."

"Oh." My confusion was culled but not completely. The sex was quite good and kept me satisfied so that I didn't even find myself eyeing anyone else up but Jason and I really hadn't added any strange requests at all. He did have a thing for slapping my ass occasionally and enjoyed taking his manhood all the way back to my throat but we hadn't crossed any severe lines.

It made me wonder what Jason had in store now.

He stood up from the bed and removed my jeans along with my briefs. Then he pulled my shirt up all the way to my neck but didn't remove it. All the while he remained clothed.

"I'm excited but I still have to ask what's going on." I said cautiously. Jason hesitated "Do you trust me?"

The question threw me off a little. It was something I hadn't actually thought about in a, well, never. Did I trust Jason? Trust to me was a luxury reserved for certain people in my life. Namely, my dad, Jay and the person who saved me and taught me how to live. In high school I obviously didn't have any friends I could trust. My brother I didn't trust for obvious reasons, my mother had lost my trust ever since she screamed at me when I came out. Even though I'd always love her and respect her, trust was something I could give her since I knew deep down I could reveal something else to make her look at me the way she did that day.

But Jason, what did I really think of Jason?

"Yes." I answered.

"Good." He said before going to the drawer next to the bed to search for something. I resisted the urge to crane my neck and take a look at whatever he seemed to be looking for but didn't so that I could enjoy the surprise the way he wanted to.

He went back to the bottom of the bed where my legs were opened and exposed and knelt there. My legs went over his shoulders and next thing I knew his hot breath fanned against my hole. Oh.

"Jason." I croaked.

"Shhh." He said assuring gently holding my left thigh "I just want to make you feel good." And with that he took a little lick at my asshole.

"Oh!" I shouted at the small but intense action. This was what he wanted. It was new and felt very good. Jason continued to lick me, slowly and torturously digging his tongue inside me only to pull out whenever I tried to rotate my hips. He gripped both of my thighs so that I could move my legs away from his shoulder but I couldn't care less about the bruises he would surely leave – all that mattered was how I was virtually losing my mind over that insane tongue of his.

"Jason." I breathed not caring how desperate I sounded.

The bastard moaned sending vibrations all the way to my cock. It laid red and neglected on my stomach gathering precome each time he hummed against me like he was enjoying a delightful sundae.

I took pleasure in the fact that I was the delightful sundae.

"Please." I begged for some release.

Some rhythm to this painful pleasure I endured. Jason, taking pity on me, grabbed my cock with one of his hands without removing his mouth from my hole. He tugged, I cried. It was a teasingly wonderful cycle.

His tongue penetrated me deeper while he frantically jerked me off faster and faster. I was surely in some sort of demented sexual paradise at this stage. Jason ate me out like I was some sort of delicious turkey buffet served out for his enjoyment. Normally most men would be repulsed at the thought of giving pleasure to their partners down there but he didn't hesitate of express disgust in any manner.

Maybe fate gave me the common sense to shower before our movie so I didn't feel as self-conscious.

"Jason more." I whined sitting up to run my hand through his hair and press him down further. I was too taken by pleasure to even care that I might be suffocating him but he didn't seem to care either because he just let me do it. I rocked my hips slowly, drawing out the feeling until Jason began jerking me off impossibly fast and before I knew it; my orgasm was ripped off like a bandage.

I screamed out coming all over his hand and riding his tongue like a madman as I came hard. Exhausted, I fell back unto the bed while Jason stood up and wiped his hand with the boxed tissues on his bedside drawer.

He smiled lying down beside me "Did you like it?"

I turned to him "Did I like it? You just ate me out and gave me the best orgasm of my life. I'm keeping you forever."

Jason's smile went wider and I noticed that he was hard in his pants. I tried to reach for it but he held my hand "No. I just wanted to do that one thing for you, no need to return the favor now."

I gave him a stern look "Sweetheart, you just rimmed me like a boss and I intend to pay my debt. Now lie down there and shut up while I give you a blowjob better than any pornstar."

"Thanks for coming." Patrick said in a grateful tone.

"Anytime." I replied stuffing my hands in my pocket. When Patrick had called to say he needed my opinion on something and didn't want Jay to find out, I had my doubts at first. Jay had still been roving on and on about Patrick's meth lab and how he was too heartbroken to know that his boyfriend was causing New Yorkers around to feed their addiction and yada, yada, yada. Later when he was drunk, he said something about always wanted to date a drug lord like in fiction and that it turned him on to know that Patrick had a dark side.

With the number of times I'd rolled my eyes, it was surprisingly that my eyes weren't stuck permanently inside my head.

But I would be lying if I said that I wasn't curious to know if what he wanted to show me had anything to do with his strange behavior.

Maybe I could finally find out the truth so that Jay would stop his annoying theories once and for all.

"Would you like some coffee?" He asked considerately. It was ten am on a Saturday and I was notorious for not getting up until at least 12 pm during the weekends. Plus it took extra effort to drag myself from bed with a naked Jason still in it.

"No it's fine." I said.

We were in Central Park where he told me to meet him before we drove out to where ever the hell he wanted to show me.

"I'm really glad that you decided to help me with this." Patrick said with a thankful smile. "It's just that his has been eating at me for months and I just want to let another person know before I kill myself with excitement.

My stomach dropped a little. Patrick wouldn't be doing anything bad would he? I'd labeled anything like that as absurd but I didn't really think hard enough to care. Was I wrong?

His expression was bright "We should start going now." I got into his Audi and we drove off.

"Where exactly are we going?" I asked cautiously.

"Connecticut." He replied excitedly. I leaned back into the comfy chair and wondered what the hell was in Connecticut.

It wasn't known for have any prominent meth labs was it?

We drove in comfortable silence for about an hour. "It's strange how to two of us don't really talk outside of Jay isn't it?" He said breaking the silence.

I shrugged "Yeah. Kind of weird when you really think about."

"He's the glue that holds me to a lot of things." Patrick said. "He's the most exciting person in the world to me." I smiled a little. Jay was an exciting little bastard to be honest.

"Jay's crazy all right." I confessed.

"You know, when we first met, he tried to attack me."

I couldn't hold in my laughter "Really? Why?" Patrick smiled "Well it was in Sydney where he was vacationing and we both happened to be in a zoo. He looked a little lost to me because he kept waving a map around so when I walked up and tapped him on the shoulder, the poor thing was so startled that he mauled me. Kept on screaming about how I shouldn't kidnap him because his family would be too annoyed to pay a ransom until I got him to calm down before he removed my eye."

I was full out giggling at this stage because I hadn't heard this story at all. Jay only told me they'd met on vacation when he was 17 but not this much detail.

"What did you do?" I couldn't help but ask.

"As soon as I calmed him down and directed him properly, he wouldn't let me go claiming he intended to pay me back for almost assaulting me by taking me to lunch. And well, as soon as I got over the shock of some crazy American teenager trying to kill me, I realized he was kind of cute."

That was a sappy romance story at its finest.

"And you've been together since." I said.

"And we've been together since." Patrick echoed. "Jay's just everything to me you know? Sometimes he's a little crazy but I love him that way. He's like the sunshine I never knew I needed in life. He's done impossible things to make me happy." He was starting to sound emotional. "So I'm going to do my best to make him happy now."

"That's amazing." I whispered.

He nodded but didn't say anything further. I'd not really taken much thought about Patrick, but he was obviously a wonderful guy who my best friend deserved.

"You're alright Patrick Stopper." I said.

He smiled "You too Ryan Perry."

We reached a residential neighborhood which confused me a bit because I wasn't sure if he was visiting someone. We stopped at a particularly large and beautiful house. It was painted yellow and had all these columns and ridges and a large yard in front.

Patrick came out of the car "This is it."

"This?" I said confused coming out of the car. "Are we visiting someone?"

He grinned "No. This is the surprise. I bought this place."

What?

"Really?" I asked stunned. Patrick nodded "It's kept me busy for a while to be honest. The basement and pipeline system was a mess but I hired a few people to help me work on it. We had to use these awful smelling chemicals to clear out the guck but it's coming along nicely."

Chemicals.

"That's why you smell like chemicals." I blurted out. It was Patrick's turn to look confused "What." I told him all about what Jay had said and his whole meth lab idea. It got Patrick laughing out loud "Really! Well I've smelled terrible because I come after work to check and work on the house with the guys I hired. The reason I don't tell him is because I want it to be a surprise for him. The money was the pay for the refurbishments and all. I'm not doing anything illegal at all. I'm not proud of lying, but I need to keep it a surprise."

"Wow." I said. "So you bought this house for him?"

"For us to move in together. He's always talked about how living in the city is fun but he's always wanted a more permanent settlement in a quiet area. He loves big suburban houses so I decided that this would be perfect after a friend from work told me about it." He explained.

"He'll love it." I said sincerely.

"That's why I wanted you here. Since you're his best friend I wanted your opinion on everything." He said rather shyly.

"Jay will adore it." I said very sure of myself. "He'll love it so much." Their devotion ached my heart a little. I wondered how it would feel to be so sure of someone the way Patrick was of Jay. It made me wonder of it could also be the same with me and Jason.

Who likes the new name and cover? Because I know I do ;).

What do y'all think of their budding relationship?

And what are these thoughts our Ryan is beginning to have?

What do you all think of the solved mystery behind Patrick's strange behavior?

My dogs watched me write that smutty scene with Ryan and Jason. I think they're judging me silently.

Chapter 13 (Greendale)

S ONG - AMERICAN CANDY - THE MAINE

"Fuck." Emmett moaned softly on top of me stiffening his entire body at his release before plopping his body next to mine in exhaustion. I opened my eyes in relief having reached my own climax a few moments ago.

"Wow that was amazing." He breathed out lying down next to me. I smiled placing my head on his bicep "You were awesome." I wasn't lying. The sex was good. Memorable even. But the awed expression Emmett had on was something I couldn't copy. So I smiled tightly instead. It wasn't earth shattering sex or anything.

"I wish we could do that all the time." He said placing his hand over mine. I shrugged "Well, reality sucks and we have normal lives to live."

"Still I wish you didn't cancel so much like yesterday." He pouted. Yesterday I had been in avoiding Gerard Coffey since he was continually blowing up my phone and threatening to find out where I lived. I knew he would because it would mean answering several questions on his part but I still stayed indoors anyway. After so many long dates, I stopped talking to him after sleeping together just twice. I didn't think it was cause such a desperate effect on him.

He'd been calling me non-stop.

"Not my fault. I had stuff to do." I said. It amused and surprised me how attached Emmett had become to me. In the beginning that was my agenda but I didn't see it coming on as smoothly as it did. He was clingy, emotionally deprived and liked to talk a lot. So much different from the Emmett Anderson I knew who always cruelly laughed whenever Nathan shoved me against a locker.

"Stay with me longer." He demanded when I tried to get out of bed. I turned back and smirked "No can do. I need to get home to study for my English test."

"Fuck that." He drawled grabbing my hand. Somehow whenever I imagined a relationship in which I had a boyfriend who didn't let me out of bed, I didn't imagine it with Emmett playing a star role. I imagined it would have been a cute, harmless guy who's fingers didn't make me inwardly squirm and whose long gazes I wouldn't end up doubting their sincerity. Not the boy who'd been my co-tormentor since I was about 14 years old.

For the longest time I'd hated him the same way I hated Nathan, painfully and explicitly. I always used to quietly hope in the midst of my tears, that one day they'd feel what the made me feel as those long tearful nights.

Now Karma had granted me a full access view to seeing it go down myself.

"I have to go." I said with a playful smile dragging my shirt from his grasp.

Emmett sighed pitifully, lying back on his pillow "Someday I'm going to make you spend the night with me."

I grunted "In a future where I don't have a curfew, yeah."

Before I could go, he leaned up and kissed me softly on the lips. Such softness I didn't think he would be capable of. Somehow it ended up reminding me of a powerful punch Nathan packed one day on my belly. I couldn't feel the difference much.

"At least shower first." He pleaded. "Do you really want to go home smelling like sex? I wonder what your parents would think." He tried for a cheeky smile but all I could think was, why do you care? You never thought of how they would feel seeing me in the bruises your best friend covered me with.

"Fine." I said with a sigh.

We had sex again in the shower. I had to promise Emmett of a whole afternoon together the very next day before he would let go home. His clinginess had made my skin itch a little. He was like a fucking five year old.

Walking out the front door of the Anderson's magnificent home, my entire body froze in shock at the sight of Nathan Coffey walking from his Jeep. His green eyes as piercing as ever and a familiar scowl made its way to his face when he saw me. In the past, the combination would have made me to start crying immediately.

"What the fuck are you doing here?!" He thundered.

I tried to hide my flinch. I wasn't the same Ryan from a few months ago, I was better, much better. He didn't have any effect on me anyway. I tilted my head forward daringly "Last time I checked this isn't your house so why do you care?"

Nathan hadn't said a single word to me since the semester began and I wouldn't begin the momentous occasion the way he expected me to. I was different – I was better now. He clenched his jaw "Well this happens to be my best friend's house. So tell me what the fuck you were doing here Ryan."

Don't let him intimidate you.

You're beautiful now.

You're invincible.

You're not afraid of him anymore.

"If you must know, Emmett and I were working on an art project. Mr. Jensen assigned us together and we have to work together so that's why I'm here." I lied smoothly. Emmett and I were in the same art class without Nathan so my lie wouldn't be so easily detected unless Emmett fucked up. It was also a good thing that I'd come here straight from school so I was still with my backpack and books if he turned out to be smart enough to think forward. I held my posture refusing to let myself be stared down by him.

"Why the hell would he pair you guys together?" Nathan asked next.

I shrugged "I don't know what goes on in his head. You'll have to ask him yourself. Anything else you want to ask?"

His eyes trailed a bit longer as if he did, but he shook his head. "I don't know what you think you are now, waltzing around school like you're some kind of sliced bread just because you did some wacked up plastic surgery. You're still nothing to me." His words almost brought a familiar sting to my chest but my newly established confidence pushed it way.

It almost made we want to tell him how special his brother and best friend thought I must have been since they'd been fucking me repeatedly for the past two months.

I smiled widely "See you around Nathan. And by the way, you're nothing to me too if you were wondering."

Without waiting for a reply, I walked to the Camry I'd been gifted a few days after turning seventeen by my Dad, got in and turned on the ignition. Someday, I swore mentally, I'll give him back the scars he gave me.

Plus the ones he made me give myself.

"Where were you?" Chris demanded when I got home. I rolled my eyes walking into the kitchen with him hot on my trail, "I'm sorry Mom. Don't you look a little different?"

His scowl showed he wasn't amused.

"Why do you care?" I asked getting myself a Diet Coke from the fridge. Before nothing would make me go near a diet anything. Now it was all I ever had. He frowned "You're always home exactly after school. Now you're two hours late and Mom isn't home yet. She'd flip if she found out."

I forcefully dropped the can on the granite countertop "Look, I don't know when you started 'caring' about what I do but please stop. It's kind of making me sick to my stomach. Go back to being broody and rude, you talked less then and I appreciated it more."

Chris looked somewhat hurt by what I said but I looked away without a care. How sweet when the roles were reversed.

"Because this isn't you Ryan."

His words made me stumble a little but I recovered "Don't even fucking go there because you have never known me. You treated me like shit in the past and I don't know what the hell you think you're doing now but don't you ever pretend you know who I am. Because you have never known that."

He was shocked but didn't say another word. I grabbed my drink and went upstairs to start my homework and hopefully immerse my mind in something else for at least an hour. As I walked up, my brother's words still rung in my mind.

This isn't you Ryan.

Who was I really? Was I this homme fatale creature I had made myself to become? Was I now a master at deceit and seduction? Or was as I really just a bitter little boy playing at revenge? Maybe if I answered those questions I would finally understand what I was doing. Or if it was all really worth it. A dark thought slithered its way reminding me that by going through with all planned, I would sell my soul in the process. People didn't do bad things to other people without being bad? Didn't they?

I pushed away the thoughts with the tallest mental bulldozer I could summon.

I feel like this was a little shitty for some reason......

Ryan has a pretty complicated past I supposed.

Chapter 14

Just to let you know, there's a bit of triggering content in this chapter so keep an eye out for it.

SONG - GOD KNOWS I TRIED - LANA DEL REY

"Hmm, repeat that one again." I hummed stretching a little with my head on Jason's chest. We were currently cuddled up in my apartment reading. Well Jason was the one reading out loud because I absolutely adored his voice. Packets of eaten Ethiopian take-out were scattered on my coffee table with a half filled bottle of wine. Jason came to my apartment with several books saying he'd been spring cleaning and found them stacked up in his closet.

At first, the thought of reading made me grimace but combined with his sultry voice and the endearing words, I was on a cloud 9.

Last week when we had dinner with Jay and Patrick, all Jay kept saying was how cute and amazing Jason was. They'd never met anyone I dated before so it seemed to speak volumes about how serious we were. Patrick had a polite smile all through dinner and with one look I knew that he hadn't told Jay about his house in Connecticut. It was only a matter of time. Besides it made me feel closer to my best friend's boyfriend that we were in on something secret for once.

Jay had cooled down on his meth conspiracy anyway. He and Jason got along like brothers. I was almost tempted to remind him about how sure he was that Jason was a serial killer in the beginning. It was nice going on a double date with my best friend and my boyfriend. It wasn't something I'd ever assumed would happen, but I was thankful for it anyway.

It seemed to further prove the hypothesis that somehow Jason and I would do good in this relationship business.

"Connaissez-vous la rose amère . Fait de la saumure et le refus. Que les fleurs sur l'océan. Dans le flux et le reflux de la marée. Comme après la pluie, l'arc-en-ciel." He recited softly, each pronunciation perfect as ever. I wondered how he learned to do so.

"That was hauntingly beautiful." I commented.

He chuckled, making his chest vibrate "You don't even know what it means."

"I'm still sure." I said stubbornly tracing my finger on his clothed chest. "What does it mean anyway?"

"Do you know the bitter rose, made of brine and refusal? That flowers on the ocean, in tidal ebb and flow, as after rain the rainbow." He translated. I hummed "I was right. It is hauntingly beautiful. When did you learn to speak French?"

"When I was younger, I had a neighbor. Mrs. Sabine, lovely woman. She moved here from Belgium and used to give me free chocolates when I'd go to keep her company. The French lessons were part of it too. Every day since I was ten years old, she taught me French until I became a fairly fluent." He explained rubbing my arm.

My handsome, incredibly talented boyfriend. Of course he could speak French too.

"That's awesome." I said. "My grandmother was Dutch and I can only say cake in Dutch. She tried to teach me but I'm hopeless at language."

"Well clearly she loved you a lot if she was willing to overlook that when it came to your inheritance." He said.

I contorted my face in confusion "What?"

"I mean she didn't care since she still gave you money right?" He explained further. I blinked remembering our earlier conversation when I lied about how I paid for my housing. "Oh yeah. She didn't really keep grudges."

"That's good." Jason commented. If he noticed my slight slip-up, he didn't say. I hoped that it wouldn't later come to haunt me. Jason and I had been dating for a fairly reasonable period of time being five months and it seemed clearer at this stage that I might need to tell him certain things about myself. Whenever he asked about several things about me, I put them off as long as I could but it was obvious that his curiosity would inflate until he practically demanded an explanation. Earnestly I hoped that it wouldn't come to that.

"Read more." I said hoping to get myself to focus on our current activity. "This haunting rose poem's got me in a mood."

Jason looked amused "Alright. Should I continue or do you want another one?"

"Continue." I muttered closing my eyes.

"Le rêve-rose l'âme-rose. Vendu dans poésies dans la rue. La gamme de couleurs-rose le jeu-rose......." His words mesmerized me. Maybe it was the language or the way he spoke it or maybe my brain had been subconsciously picking up the meaning, but it made something stir in me sweetly. I didn't want any of it to end. And not just the reading. Everything that being with Jason entailed.

I had never anticipated having a conventional relationship before. I'd always expected that I would be alone with maybe a few flings to keep me in style. It seemed ideal enough to me.

Until now.

"Kiss me." I said cutting him off.

"Oh." He looked pleasantly surprised. "Of course."

It felt good to have his lips on mine. They were warm and smooth, not chapped like the majority would expect. He hummed holding my waist to keep me in place as he pushed the book away to lie on top of me. I tangled my fingers in those luscious locks on his, hitching my leg around his waist. I shivered feeling his hardness against mine. Eyes wide shut and back arched forward, I moaned into his mouth as we rocked against each other fiercely, desperately.

He made me feel things I never knew I'd wanted to feel in the first place. Jason was so different and his difference was celebrated. I didn't care that he couldn't buy me a Maserati or let me rub shoulders with pretentious elites.

The way he touched me and treated me was enough. Like I was something worth it even though I'd never felt that way before.

His truthful confidence and rock hard persona.

He was all man. And my man.

"Should I get a condom?" Jason asked quietly. The books were scattered carelessly on the floor along with our shoes and his belt. Suddenly I didn't want that. I wanted him to hold me and cradle my head on his chest while I struggled to keep these roaring feelings in check.

I shook my head "N-No, can me not have sex? I just want you to hold me please." I expected to see some disappointment shine his handsome face. He was human after all. Most guys would accuse me of being a tease and the truly horrible ones would take it without asking.

But Jason only smiled "Of course. I don't mind."

"Thank you." I muttered cuddling him earnestly. This was the sort of needy creature I'd turned into. I didn't even like cuddling normally.

"Besides we do have a lot of sex." He added honestly. I pretended to glare "Is that a complaint I hear?"

He spluttered and I was reminded of the shy, stuttering guy I'd first been infatuated with "Oh I'm not complaining! It's great actually! Most people would be jealous because we have a lot is totally what I meant to say."

I burst out in laughter "Seriously I was only kidding. You're so cute like that."

It was not Jason's turn to glare at me "I hate you."

I winked "Not you don't babe."

His glare softened into a smile "You're right, I don't."

The statement made me heart beat a little faster. Goodness I was probably overthinking this already. He couldn't possibly mean the opposite of that statement could he?

"No one can ever hate me. I'm too lovable." I said deflecting. Something I was obviously good at.

It worked. Jason grinned "Right, I'm living proof of that aren't I?" Of course I knew that not everybody loved me. At least I knew a few people who owed a lifetime of pain and hatred towards me. I would actually feel sorry about what I'd don't to them....but I couldn't. Not ever.

As my longtime friend would say, there's no reason to feel ashamed for defending yourself. Especially when you have a good reason to defend yourself.

"Hmmm, you were reading me antsy French poetry just a little while ago." I purred.

"Louis Aragon? He's the least antsy of them all to be honest." Jason said. "For a major guilt trip, you should try Danielle Collobert or Charles Baudelaire, they were some sad people."

I stared at him.

"What?" Jason asked looking confused.

"It's so sexy how knowledgeable you are about all this." I stated seriously.

There was that blush of his "Funny you think that. In the past, I've always been seen as nerdy or boring. Not sexy."

"What? You're spouting French poetry and speaking perfect French. That's more than enough to make the whole of New York to lose their underwear."

Jason laughed "That would sound like a mass underwear revolution. I'm not sure I'm ready to lead such a movement." We giggled together like kids until I turned to face him seriously. "You're amazing and everything you do is amazing too. People like you have no reason to feel insecure."

"You too." He replied.

I smiled tightly. He didn't know the whole story behind it. He gently grabbed my left hand "Do you mind if I ask you how you got these scars?"

The question must bugged him for a while. I admired his patience for a moment. I sighed "I was in a really bad place when I was a teenager."

"Did it have to do with high school?" Jason asked carefully. Bullying.

"Mostly." I said tersely. It was more to do with the people in high school. Even though it was healed for a while now and was nothing more than a scar, sometimes it throbbed and I could feel everything that happened in that exact moment. The fear, the tears, the ways my hands shook covered in blood and the metallic smell that overtook my senses and made me dizzy. It made me clench my fist tightly.

"I'm sorry." Jason said startling me. He looked concerned, almost afraid. I felt guilty for making him worry like this.

"I'm not like that anymore." I said. I didn't need to explain what; we both knew what I meant. Obviously it wasn't so easy. There were still moments I ate a little too much and would remember the harsh taunting I used to endure. Sometimes working out in the gym I'd imagine a small whisper saying "Lard ass."

Sometimes I needed to remind myself that I wasn't 16 years old anymore. I was stronger and better now. My life had changed for the better.

I was beautiful now.

"Promise me that no matter what happens, with us, with you, you'll never think of that dark place again." Jason asked. No, he pleaded. His eyes were large and little scared and I was would dug down the stars and moon for him right then.

"I promise." I said sincerely with every fiber of my being.

Before we could kiss to sweeten the deal, my phone rang obnoxiously loud interrupting us. I groaned "What now?"

"Maybe you should answer it in case." Jason suggested obviously being the better one of the two of us.

I sighed "You're right."

It was an unknown number. I silently hoped it wasn't Chris using a clever tactic to reach me since I made it clear that a century would pass before we ever spoke again before picking up. "Hello?"

"Ryan! Don't tell me you've forgotten about me already!" a high pitched female voice spoke up. It took seconds for me to register the familiar voice "Astrid?" Jason looked puzzled but waited patiently for me to speak again.

"In the flesh honey." She laughed. "Well I will be tomorrow. I'm coming to New York and I want us to catch up on everything." It was Astrid, the first friend I'd ever made and the person who singlehandedly changed my life.

She stopped me from killing myself all those years ago.

Just to put this out, Suicide is serious and if you know anyone suffering or are suffering, please don't be along. Every single one of you is beautiful and lovely and worth something so don't ever let anyone make you think otherwise. I don't know any suicide lines but PM me because i'm always ready to talk. Bullies are cowards and people who put you down because they have nothing else better for them. Always treat people how you would love to be treated. I've been teased and bullied too and I know how terrible it felt.

On a lighter note......

singing And this is when shit starts brewing. Astrid is the person you've all been waiting to meet whether you know it or not.

chapter 15

P icture of Astrid on top.

SONG - MONEY - FOXES

Astrid was one of a kind. Gorgeous, sophisticated and with a magnetic aura, there was no avoiding her once acquainted. It would explain why she was the very first friend I'd made all those years ago and still remained very much in my life today.

"Do you have a reservation?" the host politely asked. I was in Le Meriden, a newly opened restaurant in the Upper East Side. It was semi-formal; the sort of place where suits and evening gowns weren't exactly required but you knew that dressing down would still earn you a funny look. Exactly the sort of place I expected her to pick for our lunch date.

"Yes. In the party of Miss. Armani." I replied.

He smiled at me "Follow me to your table sir."

I was led through he oddly designed establishment. It was decorated in Persian styled décor but had French phrases stenciled on the walls and half nude sculptures. He led me to a private booth shielded away from prying eyes where Astrid was seated on the low table with red cushions as chairs. She was dressed in a white wrap around jumper, her delicate wrists were encased with two diamond encrusted bracelets and a matching pair as diamond studs on her ear. Her normally short stylish hair had grown into luxurious tresses that stopped on her shoulder and were swept past her ears. I noticed a new tattoo peeking out of her white pants on her crossed ankles.

"Just a year away and you've already forgotten about me." She joked reaching out for a hug. I pecked her on both cheeks as was our customary greeting. Sometimes it struck me as a bit risqué but it was tradition.

"I can never forget about you." I said kissing her hand.

Astrid laughed waggling her finger "No wonder you get all the boys. That charm of yours is simply astounding."

I grinned sitting down "I missed you Astrid."

"Oh me too Ryan. Sometimes I wish I wasn't such a butterfly who could stay in one place. But alas I am not." She said dramatically tossing her head behind.

"You let your hair grow longer." I observed.

Astrid patted her brunette mane as if just noticing it now, "It was a bit cooler where I was and decided that I let short for much too long."

"Where did you travel to?" I asked curiously.

"Iceland. Daddy is friends with the prime minister and he hosted us." She said dismissively as the waiter came with orange looking two drinks in transparent tea cups before handing us the menus. I eyed it "What is this?"

"Jasmine chai tea. Very delicious." Astrid said drinking it all in one go before I could even sip mine. "Complimentary. Isn't this place wonderful?

I discovered it when I came into the city on Thursday. I think it's a French and Persian fusion style cuisine the owner is experimenting with."

That would explain the décor.

I sipped on the sweet tea and set it down "So what have you been up to Astrid?"

She shook her head placing both hands on the table "Nothing too interesting. How have you been Ryan?" I knew what she meant to say.

Are you ok?

Not slipping into old habits?

Confident as ever?

Astrid was the reason behind my transformation in high school.

She'd found me in Boston, sitting on a ditch with my wrists slit and ready to die. It was a horrific day; Nathan and Emmett had bullied me s normal but by the time I'd gotten home, Chris was angry and turned it right on to me. He called me all sorts of names and pushed me against the way. The worst part was that when I looked up with tears in my eyes, my mother had been standing there all through. She watched him and didn't say a word which meant she thought it was true. That was the greatest betrayal of all.

My own mother thought that I was a freak and didn't stop my brother from hurting me.

I forced myself off the floor and ran as fast as I could.

She tried to call me back but I was too blinded by hurt and pain to stop. I ran out of the house and used all the money in my pocket to take a bus to Boston. I didn't know what I was doing or where I wanted to go. All I knew was that I was ready to end it all if it meant stopping all the pain.

Wobbling off the bus, I could hear the taunts and screams in my head. The words right from when I was a freshman right till the ones said to me a few hours before. I couldn't take it anymore.

I grabbed sharp rock and roughly slit my wrists sitting a ditch and waited to die. With blood oozing from my hands and my eyesight blurry from the tears, I made peace with the fact that I was going to die there that day.

Until I heard the screech of a car.

Astrid jumped out with her then boyfriend and screamed at me to stop. I didn't understand what she was saying because I refused to listen and the pain was getting too much. They bundled me up in the car and Astrid tore off a piece of her shirt to hold down on my wound so I wouldn't bleed out. I was taken to the hospital where she lied that she was my sister because I didn't want them calling my parents.

She saved my life that day.

After that I learnt who she was. Astrid Armani-Henrik, daughter of a billionaire industrialist and a Danish prince. Her mother was featured in Forbes magazine as one of the youngest self-made female billionaires of the twentieth century. Her father was a Prince seventh in line to the throne of Denmark and founder of one of the most celebrated NGOs in the world. She was beauty, power wealth and royalty rolled up into one conveniently humble package. After we talked in her penthouse, she took me on and decided to teach me how to love myself.

During the summer we flew together to LA where I engaged in a healthy weight loss program at her and she taught me all she knew. Bought my clothes, took me to mingle with her friends who were surprisingly accommodating and immersed me completely in her world claiming I was a star she'd been fortunate to discover.

Everything I was today, I owed right to Astrid Armani-Henrik.

"Wonderful." I replied sincerely. "I'm still in NYU and still living in style if that's what you're asking."

Astrid smirked "I noticed that Versace jacket you came in strutting with. Who's the new piggy bank?" I briefly touched the lapels of my jacket. I'd bought it a week earlier and I remembered how much Jason complimented it even though he refused when I offered to buy and identical one for him.

"Ah, I have a boyfriend." I said grinning.

"Oooo, dish it up babe! Is he a banker? Lawyer? Oh let me guess, he's a politician isn't he? That jacket only came out last month. I still remember the stunning model who wore it during Fashion Week." She gushed out excitedly.

I took a deep breath "Well he's a photographer. Funny, smart, absolutely intelligent and makes me laugh all the time."

Astrid was silent.

The waiter appeared again "May I take your orders?"

She smiled at him "Of course. The lamb kebab, sabzi khordan and bacheofe stew. Also some lentil salad."

"What's sabzi khordan?" I asked.

"It's a Persian cheese platter dish." The waiter replied. I shrugged handing him back the menu "I'll have the same with her thanks and some more tea too." I wasn't really feeling the rest of the menu and I trusted Astrid enough to eat what she ate.

He nodded and left with our orders.

"A photographer? Not what I expected." She replied placing her hand under her chin "So how did you meet?"

I recounted the story to and Astrid listened in utter fascination. The food came tantalizing and hot. I plucked a bit of the cheese platter and ate it facing her. She sighed "To be honest, do you really see a future with this guy?"

I frowned chewing "Well yes. Maybe not big house in the suburbs yet but I can see myself spending a good number of years with him. Jason is amazing and wonderful and he's what I've been looking for all this time. He's right for me."

Astrid chewed thoughtfully "Ok, assuming he is the "one" for you." She made quotation marks with her fingers. "How are you going to get used to being with someone ordinary?"

"How do you mean?"

She raised both hands up "Ok. Jason is a photographer. He makes a living from doing mostly freelancing gigs now. Maybe he'll get lucky and score something permanent with the big shots like GQ or Vanity or take publicity photographs for big celebrities-"

"He doesn't want to do all that stuff permanently." I interrupted. "He wants to make real art and sell his stuff in galleries."

"Yeah. He wants to sell pictures either way. So where does that leave you? Don't quote me exactly but I don't think you can afford to consistently buy those Alexander McQueen boots you love so much on a photographer's salary. Let's face it; even if you decide to work after your degree to earn a living with your beau, you're used to this lifestyle and I can assure you that it's not easy to let go. Darling you're a prince, you're used to the finer and more pleasant things in life and it suits you well. It's something you have to consider before you're so quick to throw it all away." Astrid said spooning some of the lentil salad.

I gripped my fork a little tighter "Well I still have lots of money in my savings account. I can manage it well."

She shook her head "Darling, exactly how much money do you have in your account?"

"Close to five million." I stated. Ever since I was nineteen, I'd been saving consistently. I wasn't stupid; I knew that sooner or later my boyfriends would find someone pretty to play with and I would be tossed aside immediately so I used the opportunity mooch as much as I could. Most paid my expenses so I could afford to save the allowances they gave me. Plus my job paid quite reasonably and my parents still sent a quarter of my tuition to help me through even though they thought I was swimming in quite a few student load debts but I had none. Combining all that gave me a pretty sum to tuck away for emergencies.

I knew that Astrid wasn't saying all she said to be mean or sound haughty but it was true that I was used to luxurious things. Realistically, I did need to properly assess myself to know if I was truly comfortable being with someone who couldn't immediately provide all the things I wanted with the snap of a finger.

"Ok so that's reasonable for you Ryan. But what if Jason wants a few early tips from you?" She asked next.

"He doesn't ask me for money if that's what you think." I immediately defended. "He doesn't even know what I did to get all my money. He thinks my grandmother gave me an inheritance. Last week I offered to pay for him when we went shopping and he downright refused. Jason is an honorable guy and only takes what he feels he's earned."

Unlike you, that ugly thought reminded.

Astrid smiled "Ok. Let's say all of that is true and Jason is the angel you've told me he is, does he really know everything about you?"

I stilled.

She did have a point there. My boyfriend didn't know everything about me. In fact there was a lot I'd been lying to him about.

She ate some rice "So he thinks that you can afford your fancy apartment and clothes on what your grandmother gave you huh? Jason must really trust you a lot to just believe that. If it were me I'd look deeper."

I played around with the vegetables on my plate "He does trust me a lot." The thought made me feel horrible. He trusted the lies I'd been telling him about. He trusted them without a doubt.

"So are you ever going to tell him?" She asked.

I placed my hand on my forehead "Astrid I'm not so sure to be honest. He's a really good guy. What if I mess this up by telling him the truth about the real me?"

She placed her hand on mine in comfort "Ryan, I'm not saying he's not good enough for you or he's not rich enough but I want you to look at everything without those cloudy "in love" eyes for a moment. You're my greatest friend in the whole world and I'm yours. We've both seen each other at our best and worst. If you really want your new relationship to be built on something good and solid then properly look at the facts and tell him the whole truth about yourself. That way you'll know for sure that nothing is in the way of your happiness."

"I will." I said. The once delicious saffron rice I'd been eating now tasted like sawdust. Astrid was right and I hated it completely.

This was my first real dose of reality.

Ahh, shit's getting real isn't it?

What do you think of Astrid?

Do any of you make banners or fanart? If you do, send it over and let me post it! I've been getting fond of those recently.

Chapter 16

SONG - MY LOVE - MAJID JORDAN

"Avocados? Are they on the list?" Jason asked me playfully juggling to medium sized avocados in both hands. I giggled reaching out and picking only one to place in my trolley "Yes but stop playing with those we're in public."

He spun around throwing the rejected Avocado back into the pile "You're a party pooper Ryan."

I rolled my eyes "Because I didn't let you play with the cauliflower?"

He faked a pout "I was just touching not playing with them. Don't accuse me just because you're cute."

"My being cute has nothing to do with this." I defended. He had a devilish gleam in his eyes "Yes it does."

"What-" but before I could finished my sentence, he'd pressed his lips over mine for half a second.

"Sneaky." I said simply while stacking some Rice Krispy treats into the trolley.

"Cute." He said sticking out his tongue.

I laughed pecking his cheek "No playing around or we'll never finish up grocery shopping."

Jason sighed dramatically "If we must."

When he volunteered to go shopping with me, I expected more help and less goofing. But the truth was that I truly didn't mind either way. Spending time with Jason doing anything was enough for me. After my lunch date with Astrid, I'd been a little too anxious and very nervous. Jason had noticed but I managed to give excuses for my behavior. She was right; if I really was serious about Jason and willing to take this further than my previous relationships, I needed to tell him everything about myself.

The good, the bad and the ugly. Especially the ugly.

"Can we get some yogurt too?" Jason asked.

"Sure. Why?"

"Because I want to make something special back at your apartment for us." He replied with a smile.

My heart fluttered little "With yogurt?"

"I'll have you know that there's a lot you can do with yogurt." He frowned playfully. I rolled my eyes "Alright, I won't question you Gordon Ramsey."

I turned back to pick some cereal but I felt a light tap on my butt. He just smacked my ass. I faced him incredulously "Jason?!"

"What?" He asked innocently.

"You're going to get us kicked out from here." I whisper-yelled. My face was as red as a tomato.

"Relax babe." He said crowding my space. "We have rights." I couldn't deny the fact that his naughtiness turned me on but it was inappropriate where we were. I was sure that none of the moms who shopped here frequently would appreciate the sight of two young men with hard-ons.

"Not the right to scar innocent children we don't." I deadpanned. "And you've much more touchy than normal. Anything the matter?"

He shrugged "Just trying to be more attentive if it will get you out of the funk you're in."

His reply made me smile. It was great to be with a guy who made me smile the way Jason did. This was all the more reason that I couldn't lose him.

Jason just smiled "You're amazing."

Then it all came crashing down in my head. I wasn't amazing. He only saw the front I decided to put up as amazing. If he knew the real me, he wouldn't think so. The guilt pressing through me was so heavy.

"We should get the yogurt." I said instead walking towards the fridge. He looked confused at my behavior but decided to leave me be "Um ok then. I'll just get some peas and pasta too."

"You do that." I said avoiding eye-contact. We walked in opposite direction and I went to pick out the yogurt. I'd gotten two jugs of milk before I realized that I didn't ask Jason what kind of Yogurt he wanted. I stood for about two minutes wondering whether to pick sweetened or plain before inevitably placing both into the trolley.

"Ryan?"

I turned to see the face of a familiar acquaintance.

"Jon?" I echoed.

He – Jon – grinned in the s0.alacious manner I'd always remembered about him. His formerly black hair was dyed light blond and he'd lost a few pounds. Not that he was out of shape previously. Now he was more lean muscle than severe eight pack which I thought suited him better.

"What a coincidence. The world is truly a small place." He exclaimed.

"Yes it is." I replied politely. "It's been what, 2 years now?"

"Exactly that and I see you haven't changed much. Still as gorgeous as ever." He said and I remembered exactly what a flirtatious creature he was.

Jon Hummer was one of the first men I ever "dated" and one of the only few ones I'd parted from quite civilly. A wealthy hedge fund manager, he indulged me on the side to satisfy his wilder pleasures while keeping up appearances with his socialite wife. Unlike most of the men I'd been with, he wasn't gay but pansexual and had a terrible weakness for not being able to keep it monogamous. With him it was easier to break off when the cutoff point was reached and there were no hard feelings. Jon was certainly the sort of man who didn't get jealous when he felt that there were others who'd easily have him.

"And you're still great at flattering." I said. "Shopping for the house? I thought errands were beneath you like you always claimed."

Jon smiled "Still a great memory. Unfortunately I'm obliged since my daughter is throwing the biggest tantrum known to man unless I get her some ice-cream."

"You have a daughter?" I asked surprised.

He nodded proudly "Yes. Two years old and the light of my life." It was hard to picture the Jon Hummer I knew as a father. The man liked to throw toga parties and fuck people against his wall-to-ceiling windows with his fiancée sleeping in the next room for goodness sakes. Hopefully his wife balanced out his partying tendencies.

"That's great." I said in expected politeness. "Sorry but I've got to go. Don't want to keep my boyfriend waiting."

"Ah, so who's the lucky cow this time?" I knew he was teasing but it still sent all the wrong sorts of emotions right through me. Jon used to joke all the time about how I reminded him of a milkman. Sucking poor cows until they were dry. It was a mystery how we ended on a good note.

I curled my lip "He's not a cow. We've been together for a while and if you're asking, I don't do that any longer."

Now it was Jon's turn to be surprised "Really? Ryan Perry's given up his long time profession. Never thought I'd see the day."

I held in the urge to grip my teeth "Well now you have."

"So what's this lucky guy's name?" He asked with a shit eating grin.

"Jason and he's a photographer." I said trying to exude the pride that I felt on the inside. Jon only smiled "I have a feeling you won't be with his Jason the photographer very long?"

"And why's that?" I asked turning to see him properly.

"Because you can't stand ordinary my dear. You never could. Let's face it Ryan, you're not the type to slum it eating take out all day while cuddling with your boyfriend in some shit hole of an apartment. You deserve to sip champagne on yachts, dine in only the finest restaurants and live right above the sky. You're only fooling yourself."

"I'm not and you don't know a single thing about us." I said not even trying to keep the anger out of my voice. "And he's not ordinary at all."

This was his edge, pushing me to the extreme. It always gave Jon some kind of thrill to push his partners to their limit. But sadly for him I wasn't his partner anymore.

"But I do." He said with that grin of his again. "I know everything about you Ryan and I know that people don't change. So whatever starving artist romantic fantasy you have now just enjoy it while you can because it'll be over before you know it and you'll go back to living life the way you know best."

"As wonderful as it was to see you I should get going." I said already pushing my cart away. Before I could move forward Jon gently grabbed my arm and placed his business card on my palm.

"For old times' sake." He said with a wink.

I nodded stiffly making sure that I walked two steps forward and tore it up right in his line of sight before tossing it on the floor. Maybe the person who cleaned up the aisle would find it much more useful that I did.

"You got the yogurt?" Jason asked when I rolled the cart for him to put his items in.

"Yep." I said with a smile.

"Alright then." He said looking slightly dubious as my change in mood. We paid for the items and went back to my apartment. True to his word, Jason made some sort of chicken Caesar salad using yogurt for dressing to go with the lasagna. At first I was doubtful about his concoction but I was proved wrong once I realized how good it was.

"Never doubt me." Jason said when I was packing up the dishes.

I rolled my eyes "It was just dumb luck this time."

He laughed "Just admit that I am a whiz at everything I do. Here let me help with those." He helped my place some dishes into the sink.

"Such a gentleman." I teased.

"Well I was raised well." He replied. Leaning on the kitchen granite, I eyed him "What was your mom like?"

"Sweet, caring and funny as hell. Not afraid to fry out my ass if I was wrong but all in all, a very good woman." Jason replied washing up some dishes and putting the rest in the dishwasher.

"Must have been a great person to raise you." I commented. He smiled wistfully, as though trying to reminisce on something good "She is. Amazing too, you'd both get along like two peas in a pod. I can't wait for you to meet here."

"You'd want us to meet?" I stuttered through.

"Yes." He said with conviction coming towards me. "It would actually be great."

I turned away from him and focused on the dish cloth as if it were the most interesting thing in the world. I couldn't keep lying to him, I just couldn't.

"Jason." I started with a solemn tone. "There's something I have to tell you."

"Um, not bad news I hope?" Jason asked nervously. I shrugged "Not really sure how to define it."

"You're not sick are you?" He asked going from nervousness to panic. I shook my head suddenly wishing that I was sick at the moment. That would be a lot better than what was going to come.

"I-I....." I took a deep breathe. "I fuck men for money." The atmosphere went tense so fast. Jason was silent and I couldn't dare to look him in the eye. The silence was deafening.

What was he thinking right now? Was it really bad? What was he going to say?

"Is this a joke?" He said finally.

I bit my lip "I wish that I was joking."

"So are you a prostitute? Is that it?"

Words had never stung me so hard before. I choked on my words "Jason it's not like that."

"Then how? How is it Ryan?" He shouted. I'd never heard him raise his voice at me before. It didn't like it one bit. This wasn't the Jason I knew.

"I'm not a prostitute." I said in a whisper of a voice.

"You just said that you sleep with men for money." He stated.

I folded my hands together "I get with rich men sometimes to pay my bills and buy me things, sort of like a kept boy. I've been doing it since I was 18 but I stopped right when I met you. I swear that I didn't mean to lie to you Jason, I swear it. It was just hard to find the right time to tell you."

"So what? Have you been with them since we were together? Have I been taking turns to fuck you while other men do the same?" Jason asked but he didn't sounds angry now. He sounded broken. "Were you just playing with me on the side?"

"No!" I shouted. "I was never and will never play around with you Jason. My feelings for you are real, I swear. I haven't been with anyone since we got together."

"How can I know that?" He asked. "How can I know who you really are?" I kept quiet because I didn't know how to answer that truthfully. I desperately wanted him to believe me, to believe that I had changed for him.

"Tell me the truth Ryan; your grandmother didn't leave this place for you did she?" He asked quietly. I hesitated "No she didn't. I've never met her to be honest."

"Fuck." He muttered. "How did you pay for it?"

"My ex-boyfriend got it for me." I replied feeling shame creep in. Jason lowered his head as though he was just trying to process everything I'd just said. The funny thing was that saying what I just did never made me feel ashamed with anyone else but with Jason I wanted to be better. I wanted to be someone he wouldn't feel conflicted about it.

"I've changed Jason. I changed for you, for us." I said desperately trying to make him see reason. I walked closer to him but he raised a single hand to show that he didn't want me to come closer. It hurt to think that he didn't even want to be next to me.

"I can't give you fancy things. Fuck, I can't even afford all those fancy clothes you love or take you to parties so I don't even know why you're with me." He whispered. "I'm not rich. I'm not your type so.....maybe.....maybe we shouldn't be together anymore."

The words shattered me right from the inside out. He couldn't mean what he just said.

"I think we should break up." Jason said looking down.

I didn't even realize that I was crying right until I felt two hot drops on my hand. I wiped them facing Jason with my blurry vision "Please don't do this to me. I've changed, I've changed for you. You're the first person I've ever been in a decent relationship with and I don't want to lose us."

"But why does it feel like I don't even know who you are? How am I sure that you won't get bored of me since I don't have any money to spend?"

Because you're worth more than money, I wanted to scream. My throat was clogged up and all that came out of me were little choking sobs.

"It was nice meeting you Ryan." He said before finally letting himself out of my apartment for what I assumed would be the last time. When I heard the door close I fell against the sink and let out a loud sob. The dish cloth fell right along with me.

He left. He was gone.

Scrambling my phone out of my pocket, I called the only people I knew would help me in this moment.

"Hello?" Jay's smooth voice answered.

"He's left me." I cried. "Jason left me."

Someone tell me if this thing went too fast because I feel like it did.

Chapter 17

- -

Everyone seemed to hate me during the last chapter like wow.

SONG - IF I GO - ELLA EYRE

P.S I LOVE ELLA EYRE.

About twenty minutes later, Jay and Astrid burst into my apartment with Patrick trailing behind them. Immediately they set to work: Patrick went to clean up the remnants of my kitchen while Astrid and Jay worked together to carry me off the floor where I'd been sitting down absently since Jason had left. I wondered how Astrid knew since I only sobbed on the phone to Jay but he must have been the one to call her.

Either way I was grateful.

After I was successfully dumped on the couch and the kitchen was clean, Astrid brought out a bucket of Rocky Road ice cream and expensive white wine which I tore through the second it was handed to me.

Patrick shoved in a rented rom com which I could hardly pay attention to since my eyes were more blurry than often. No one said anything. They were waiting for me to say something first. I respected that.

"I told him." I said solemnly after the movie had gone halfway and I couldn't take it anymore.

"Jason?" Astrid asked tentatively.

"I told him a-and he couldn't take it." I sniffed remembering the incident. "He broke up with me." It was then that I finally recounted everything that happened. From when we were together in the supermarket with Jon to when we got home and tragedy struck.

"Oh Ry." Jay said sympathetically rubbing my shoulder. "It's not your fault."

"He said that he couldn't take care of me the way I would have wanted. I tried to tell him all I wanted was him." I said feeling the tears run down my face. I ate a spoonful of ice cream and felt remarkably settled for about a second. No wonder people turned to ice cream to cure their heartbreak.

"Well he's a bastard and a half for not listening to you." Jay concluded. "And I may have liked him in the past but no one breaks my Ry's heart."

"Thanks." I whimpered with a mouth full of the cold confectionary.

Astrid sighed pouring herself some wine "From the way you described him, I honestly expected his reaction to be a little different. You don't need someone who goes running at the first sight of your past."

"He didn't leave because he was ashamed of me." I argued. "Jason broke up with me because he was unsure. I'm not trying to defend his actions because it was a shitty thing to do and I'm here eating an entire bucket of unhealthy ice cream to drown my sorrows because I do think it was a shitty thing to do. But in understand why he acted so rashly. I would have done the same thing."

"I disagree. No one makes a decision that hastily. He must have been looking for a reason to run in my opinion." Jay argued.

"We don't know that." Astrid piped up. "We're not in his head. We don't know what he was thinking at all."

"Maybe but I sense that he was spooked out and ran out of the situation as quickly as he could." Patrick said surprising us all.

"Yeah but he did it in a douchebag way." Jay said turning to his boyfriend. "Even if he was spooked he could have handled it better."

"Most times people just go with their instincts but we can't blame them for acting irrationally." He replied.

"Jeez babe, when did you become a shrink?" Jay asked sarcastically. It was quickly becoming quite tense between the two of them.

"The important thing is that we're all here for Ryan now." Astrid said before the two lovebirds could start in a less than tamed disagreement between each other. Just because my relationship was now wrecked didn't mean I wanted the same for them.

"Thanks guys." I muttered leaning my head on Jay's shoulders. At least I had friends who were willing to drop anything at a moment's notice during my time of need.

"Anytime." Astrid replied softly. Jay patted my blonde head "At least I got to watch you experience your first heartbreak which I never thought would happen in a thousand years."

I let out a weak giggle despite myself "It's not heartbreak unless you're in love. I'll just call this a relationship disappointment." No one said anything after me. Maybe they all thought I was lying to myself but I wasn't. Even though what I felt for Jason was quite strong, it wasn't love. At least not on my end. On his end, I'll never know now.

All I knew was that at least I wasn't in love with Jason. That would have made things so much more worse.

It was two days after Jason had left and Astrid refused to let me wallow alone in my own misery. After my classes for the day she took me out shopping, a treat on her. At first I didn't want to go but the promise of new Burberry and Galliano manage to get me off my couch.

"Maybe we should get you a makeover." Astrid suggested after we left the store.

"Why?" I asked her sipping my banana smoothie.

"Just a change." She said casually shrugging.

"No thanks." I replied. I knew exactly what she was doing. Astrid had assumed that getting immersed in a project would take my mind of my devastating break up but it couldn't be more incorrect. Trying to focus on something else only reminded me how much it hurt and I wanted to avoid that. Just going with the flow seemed to work well for me.

"So what's with guy who's been shadowing us?" I asked.

Astrid made a noise of annoyance and looked behind us at the man casually dressed in a shirt and jeans who'd been following us since we left my place. "He's a bodyguard. Daddy said I wouldn't be going around without at least four anymore since I almost got kidnapped in Abu Dhabi."

"Abu Dhabi? Thought that place was fairly peaceful." I mused.

"Apparently some people entertain the thought that you can get rich by kidnapping a member of the Danish royal family." She said with a scoff as though the very idea was absurd as we walked towards the food court. "It wasn't very serious but my parents refuse to take any chances."

Sometimes I forgot exactly who Astrid was. It was easy to especially for someone who'd seen her eat a whole large sized pizza by herself, burp in the movies and could live in a large t-shirt for days without shame. But it was during moments like these or whenever I heard her speak Danish on the phone or casually speak of meeting prime ministers and presidents that I remembered exactly who Astrid was.

To her the difference wasn't so much. She could go to bed one day after dirtying herself at an animal shelter and still wake up the next day to have tea with Bill Gates or something. If there was anything to admire about her, it was the fact that she was down to earth yet powerful at the same time. Humble but the very height of sophistication.

"He's been taking his job seriously." I commented when we sat to grab some coffee.

She dropped her phone on the table "Not seriously enough if we were able to make him quite easily. I bet I could flip him over with one finger."

I laughed "Hey, not everyone can be as gifted in Krav Maga as you are."

She grinned with a tinge of pride "Well that's true. Mommy makes sure I only have the best teachers. Still can't beat her in a fight though."

Oh yeah and it was hard to ignore the fact that her mother was an actual badass apart from business guru. Once she tipped me just for the fun of it the second time we met. It made me wonder what she would have done if I was dating her daughter.

"I'm going to Tiffany's to look around. Want me to get you something?" Astrid asked once our orders arrived.

I bit into my muffin "Sure. Maybe a few clip-ons."

She nodded "Of course."

When she left I glanced at my phone and I felt a surge of indecisiveness. I hadn't called Jason since but I wanted to. I wanted to explain everything to him, to assure him that I wanted us. But then my finger always ended up hovering over his number but I couldn't press call.

You're stupid for thinking it could ever work, a voice in my head snickered. You don't do relationships Ryan, you do business deals. The dumbest thing you could ever do is think you could really give someone your heart.

Had I really been fooling myself to think that we would work?

Was it all just a fantasy?

I'd convinced myself that I was an unbreakable realist that maybe when I started dreaming, I didn't even realize it.

Was that all this was? A dream?

"Excuse me." A voice broke me away from my thoughts. Standing in front of me was the man from the boutique where I worked. Cornelius was his name I think.

"Hi." He said with a smile. "Quite fancy bumping into you here." He looked exactly the same expect his hair was a few shades darker than it was previously and he was dressed much more casually in a pair of dark jeans and a toffee colored blazer.

"Yes but it is public mall so I don't rate it as much of a coincidence as you might think." I replied placing a hand under my chin.

Cornelius cocked his head to one side "Have to say that out of many people I could bump into, I prefer you."

I sipped my coffee looking down at the table "I'm flattered."

He glanced around "May I join you? If you're alone that is."

I hesitated "I came with a friend but she's busy so maybe you can sit keep me company till she comes back." There was no harm in it I was sure.

He sat down on the chair opposite to me "So what brings you here?"

I laughed "What brings anyone to the mall? I wanted to shop. What brought you here if I may ask?" Cornelius just smiled "My niece is turning seven and the little thing is already making ludicrous demands for a birthday present."

I grinned "Cute. I was right when I said you have a thing for demanding women."

"Not just women I'm afraid." He said making a blush a little as I recalled our conversation that day. I ate another piece of my muffin when he said "You know I was rather disappointed when you didn't call me back."

I noticed Astrid's bodyguard still flanking around me. He must have stayed while the others followed her to the jewelry store. It sent a tiny piece of joy in my heart knowing that she may have wanted me protected.

"I hardly take you for a man who sits waiting all the day by the phone." I teased.

"Ah yes but I'm allowed to be disappointed when I chat with an attractive young man and he doesn't call me back." He countered and I bit my lip wondering exactly what to say next.

"I just came out of a relationship." I replied to play it safe. I wasn't even sure if it could be described as such since we had only been together for almost five months but Jay had assured me that it was correct. Hard to believe I'd never really been in an actual honest relationship before Jason.

Not so honest though, my mind reminded me. "I assumed you were also in a relationship yourself with that woman in the store."

He sighed "Yes but not with her. I was dating her sister."

My eyes widened in surprise but I refused to let it show "She seemed.....free with you." My muffin was only halfway eaten which meant I might have to order another before the conversation was over.

Cornelius grinned as though I wasn't insinuating that he was cheating with his girlfriend's sister and I noticed the attractive element in it "That is a particular trait of hers though. We were close but not that close I assure you. I believe in monogamy."

"That's good." I said with as much enthusiasm as I could muster "So you broke up?"

"Yes." He replied. "Too many differences to resolve."

"I'm sorry." I said because it was the polite thing to do. He waved his hand "Don't apologize since it wasn't your fault. So am I safe to assume that you're single?"

I sighed absently dumping some more sweeteners into my coffee. Suddenly it didn't taste quite as sweet anymore "I – it was messy and I'm not sure if I'm ready to be with someone then." It seemed like no one would ever be as good as Jason. He was far too good to measure to anyone else.

Far too good for even you, the voice whispered again. He deserved someone who wasn't as tainted as me. Someone who didn't come with so much baggage. Someone who wasn't so tainted.

"I'm not asking you to do that right now." Cornelius said leaning forward across the table. His hand lightly brushed mine. "But when you are ready, I will be waiting."

I chuckled lightly "You may wait a long time."

"Anyone can wait a long time for something good." He replied holding my hand. I should have pulled away but I didn't.

"I'm not a good thing." I said almost sharply.

But Cornelius didn't look deterred at all "Good things are always in the eye of the beholder Ryan."

"How did you know my name?" I asked not caring about how defensive I sounded. He brushed my hand with his thumb "I came into the store and asked around when you weren't on a shift. Your colleagues told me."

I swore under my breath. Hopefully if I had a stalker one day, they wouldn't meet my co-workers.

"I can give you so many things. Anything you ask for." He persuaded. I shook my head "I've heard that offer so many times. It doesn't move me."

"No you haven't been offered anything like this." He replied with his eyes still trained on me. "All you've had are men who've treated you like side puppy only worthy of being tossed their leftover crumbs. They act like they're giving you a favor with all they do yet you measure more than the partners they parade around. You're not a secret, you nothing to be ashamed of or hidden in silence. You're a not a side character my darling but the fucking star of the show and I intend to make you that. To give you everything you've always dreamed of. To make you the number one for once."

I couldn't reply after what he said to me. I couldn't even find it within myself to speak. I just sat there with my heart beating as fast as it had ever done before.

"I'll let you think about it." He said standing up with ease and grace "I trust you still have my number?"

"Yes." I stammered out.

He kissed my hand "Then I believe I will see you around."

I couldn't get my mind off what had happened. Even when Astrid came back and we left the mall, my mind was spinning around Jason and Cornelius. Jason had gone for good it seemed, he couldn't handle who I was and frankly he deserved better than me. But I wanted him back because I was selfish and craved for everything I couldn't have.

Several hours later, I lay in my bed with a text book I was trying to study and Cornelius's card lying innocently on my comforter.

He's exactly what you deserve, it whispered. You can go back to life as normal, no need for these complications.

I couldn't help but drift to thoughts of Jason once again as I clenched the card.

You don't deserve him. He deserves someone better, someone without enemies and someone normal.

I held my phone, unsure of what to do.

He deserves someone who's not a whore like you.

Twenty minutes later I found myself dialing the number on the card and asking for Cornelius Verde.

Cornelius is such a smooth fucker sliding into Ryan like that.

Does anyone hate Ryan yet? I honestly hope not.

Chapter 18

- -

C ornelius on top! Yum.

SONG - KISS IT BETTER - RIHANNA

"Mr. Verde is currently unavailable right now but I could take a message for him." The polite secretary answered me.

"Thank you. You can just tell him I called I think." I croaked to her before tossing my phone as soon as the call ended. I'd tried Cornelius's personal cell twice but it didn't go through. After that I called his office line with both fingers crossed. Normally I'd object to contacting an official line but after our meeting it felt like I just had to speak to him and he wasn't picking up his personal line.

I sighed lying down to face the ceiling. Maybe it was just a mistake, he probably didn't mean it. I could tell when someone was playing around. I'd done it to so many people after all. Flirt around during lunch time at the mall because you've got nothing better to do.

I was such a fool.

"More than once lately." I muttered to myself. It was already dark outside, almost six in the evening and I was alone. Astrid invited me for dinner but I declined claiming I was fine all by myself. The truth was that I wasn't fine but I didn't want to convince myself that I was too desperate to be alone. Jay would have happily come but Patrick was planning a dinner for the two of them. He must have been planning to tell Jay about the house.

I could survive this. I would survive this.

After all, people go through painful and awful break ups every day. Hollywood was surely making money off the concept.

But how many people nursed the idea that they could have a future with someone that they didn't deserve? Jason was ideal, almost perfect, but he and I were in two different spheres of life. Yes, his break up was hasty and he didn't listen to me explain but the truth was what was I really going to explain to him?

I'm a bit fucked up in the head because of my time as a teenager and despite all the help Astrid gave me I still feel like the way to justify my existence is by fucking and discarding men for money and many people find it a bit messed up that I've embraced the label of being a whore so proudly that it sounds more like a compliment than an insult to me. But with you I want to discard everything that I am and become someone new because you make me feel new Jason. I want to be someone better for you, someone not fucked up.

But in the end we can never get what we truly want because that's the way the world works. Jason deserved better than me.

I sighed again forcing back tears and looked outside the window from my king sized bed.

It was too fucking dark.

I was startled awake around 7:17 pm. My mouth was dry and I was a little hungry but ignored both in favor of the incessant ringing that came from my phone. Despite the fact that my eyes were still heavy from sleep I was able to discern that it was a familiar number.

"Hello?"

"Ryan?"

It was him. It was Jason. How badly I wanted it to be him oh goodness.

"It's me Cornelius." I snapped back to reality. Despite my light disappointment I smiled. I lay back on my bed "Oh hi. Thought you didn't want to talk to me after all."

"I'm very sorry if you got that impression. I was just really held up in my office and couldn't take any calls. My secretary told me you called just now and I had to reach you." He explained apologetically.

"It's ok." I replied assuring him. Probably shouldn't have judged so quickly. The relief I felt was quite evident.

"If it's any consolation I was quite annoyed that I didn't get to call you as soon as I wanted. My sister came around and she always has quite a penchant for dramatics. We fought." He said.

"I'm sorry."

"No need. She's an attention seeking bitch to be honest." Cornelius said bluntly and I found myself wanting to laugh at this declaration. It sounded mean but I just couldn't help it. Guess we must have had something in common when it came to siblings.

"If it's any consolation to you I did feel a little disappointed when I thought you wouldn't call." I flicked my nail.

"Just a little?" His voice was curious.

"Yes. Although it could turn into more if I was thoroughly convinced that there was something worth missing." I purred. At that moment it felt like I couldn't help it, teasing and flirting was too much of a second nature to me.

"I see. Perhaps I could convince during dinner?" He offered.

"Dinner sounds good." I agreed crossing my legs together on the bed.

"Is right now alright for you?" Cornelius asked. I blinked "Tonight?"

It was already dark outside. Not too late, maybe there would be a few restaurants that one could visit without a reservation. But my face was dried with tears and I felt a little weary so it didn't feel like a good option.

"I could pick you up right now if you're not busy." He offered.

"Not tonight." I replied hastily. "But tomorrow I could clear my schedule and make sure that I'm free enough to meet up with you."

"Alright." Cornelius sounded delighted either way. "Send me your address and I'll get a car to pick you up tomorrow by eight pm. I'm looking forward already."

"Me too." I said with only half honesty.

After I disconnected the call, I reevaluated my actions. Was it much too fast for me to start seeing someone else? Jason and I had been barely broken up for a week and I'd already answered the first proposition I'd been given. Didn't sound like proper break up etiquette. However, no one could accuse me of being a slut or something because, well, it was obvious enough and I didn't care.

But a part of me was worried that hurrying to date again would mean that I didn't care about Jason. I did, far too much in fact.

We just weren't good together.

I wasn't good for him.

Or so I'd convinced myself.

Beside me on my bedside drawer was a tiny fish figurine Jay gave me for my birthday some years back. It was a single blue fish leaping out, eyes wide and focused. Not a care in the world. Fish were so lucky. All they had to do was eat and swim and avoid sharks and fishermen all day long. They didn't have much to complicate their lives.

It was times like these that I wished I was a simple little fish. Because sharks and fishermen sounded easy compared to being a human being.

"I'm so glad that you agreed to this." was the very first thing Cornelius said to me when got into his car.

"Me too." I said with a smile.

Previously, I'd spent thirty minutes having a mini meltdown about what to wear and if I actually wanted to do this. I had to call my friends for a little support before making any decisions.

Jay said yes. The only thing was that I suspected that he wanted me to move on from Jason as quickly as possible to release myself from the pain. Astrid gave a huge pause first before she finally said that a date wouldn't hurt. Then she told me to wear the crème colored D&G blazer that was folded around the sleeves.

If there was anything I could count on Astrid for, it was fashion advice.

"You look gorgeous." He complimented.

"So do you." I replied and I meant it. While Cornelius was of a much older age group than the men I usually dated (excluding the English Lord and super handsy diplomat), he was handsome in an established, clean cut way.

Not like the usual twenty something year old playboys I was with but a quiet, creeping sort of charming attractiveness that made you look whether you wanted to if he passed by you.

"What restaurant would you like to go to tonight?" He asked softly. His hands were creeping on top of mine and I let in a gust of air before allowing it to remain there "You didn't make a reservation?"

"No. I actually made three."

Wow.

Cornelius grinned "The fun part is making you guess one of the three to visit tonight." I did not previously sense an eccentricity in him but I liked it a lot.

I glanced at his driver who remained stoic at our conversation then back at him "Hmm, not even a little clue?"

"I'm a fair man so I'll give you three: Sashimi, Cassulet and Biryani." He grinned. I raised my chin "There must be a thousand places in city to get those."

"But where would you think I would go?" Cornelius enquired. I tilted my head to think then it came to me almost immediately "Le Perigord. 52nd street Manhattan. If I remember correctly they serve excellent Cassulet."

"That's right." He said obviously surprised. "How did you guess it?"

I shrugged "They serve the best Cassulet in the city from my knowledge and I guessed that you must like it a lot to mention that particular dish. Just like I now know that you have a taste for Sashimi and Biryani. Japanese and Indian."

"Your observational skills astound me each time." He said lightly brushing my cheek with his thumb making my breathing hitch just a little "It's nice to have someone who actually cares enough to observe anything about me."

"No one you've dated does?" I asked.

He gave me a blank look "What do you think?"

I leaned closer to him and pretentiously whispered in his ear "I think we have a lot in common then." Then pressed my lips on his for half a second. It gave the desired effect because he was flustered and off guard much to my delight.

Seemed like I hadn't gone rusty at all.

Dinner was pleasant enough.

Cornelius was respectful, interesting and sexy as hell. He treated me well and never once did he hang me off like a trophy much to my surprise. Whenever I went out with any of the men I was with, most of them made a point of holding my waist, pulling me close or anything to indicate I was with them and they were damn proud to show it off.

Cornelius always stayed close enough but respected my personal space. He only held my hand after asking for permission and I was glad that we didn't really get any stares where we were. Living in New York was great like that.

"To be honest, I feel bad for the man who let you go." He said in the elevator to my apartment. I tensed a little at the mention of Jason "Yeah. Don't really want to talk about it."

"My bad." He apologized sincerely.

When it stopped, he held my arm pulled me towards him after we came out. I was pressed against his chest. His arm went around my waist and lips were not too many inches away from mine. Anyone who came out and saw us would get a very suggestive picture.

"Forgive me if I'm being too forward but I can't think of anything but kissing you. I've been holding myself all night long but it's been much too hard." Cornelius muttered.

I smiled "What if I said, that I really want you to kiss me too?"

"I'd say thank you and not waste any more time." And with that his lips pressed against mine in the roughest kiss I'd ever experienced. He was strong and determined. My arms involuntarily went around his neck and his grip on my waist became even tighter.

We kissed for about two more minutes before the demand for oxygen became greater. I pulled away with a pant while Cornelius brushed his thumb against his red lips.

"I want to see you again." He said. It wasn't asking or telling; it was pleading now. Without saying anything, I kissed him again for a shorter period of time.

"Ok." I said.

He grinned giving me one more kiss before backing away to the elevator. I walked to my apartment with a small smile on my face and my heart thumping in my chest until I stopped dead in my tracks at the sight of the person standing there. He smiled shyly at me just the way I remembered.

"Jason."

"I'm sorry Ryan." He said immediately.

My loves now meet again!

Thoughts?

Chapter 19

This came sooner than I expected though....

SONG - UNDERGROUND - ADAM LAMBERT

p.s I love Adam Lambert! Shameless glambert.

"Jason." I breathed out again.

He was here. Standing in front of my apartment with his hands stuffed in his pocket and expression as shy as I remembered. Fuck I wanted to kiss him so much. To hold him again. To be with him. To kiss him.

Right after sucking face with Cornelius and people wonder why you're a self-proclaimed slut, my subconscious cheerfully spoke.

"You should be punching me." He said detached.

"What?" I was confused.

Jason cleared his throat "On the way over here, I imagined meeting you up and receiving the most painful punch ever. I even carried a bandage with me."

Despite myself I couldn't help but laugh at what he'd said. He smiled too "Will I need it?"

I sighed sobering up "Wanna come in?" I didn't wait for an answer before unlocking the door and entering. He followed me walking carefully, like he was afraid that something would come up to bite him. Like I had set up some sort of trap for him to get ensnared right into. If only he knew. Somehow if there was any trap, it would be for me.

Tossing my keys into the bowl in the kitchen, I went up to my cupboards "Want something to drink?"

"No thanks." He replied. I shrugged grabbing a whole bottle of Tequila and a shot glass. Something told me that this was going to be a conversation best endured not sober. After I threw one shot down, head tilted back and buzzing pleasantly, I nodded "I'm ready."

A lie.

Deep inside of me it felt like I wasn't going to be ready for whatever he had to say.

"There's no need to explain that I'm a douche or a complete idiot, I know that already. The way I reacted was wrong in so many ways. I just let some deep fears in me take over my reasoning and cloud my judgment. I'm sorry for that." He said softly. My spine stiffened. This was not what I was expected. Most men know they're wrong but because they're proud douches, you still need to point it out to them exactly.

"What fears?" I asked. My standing behind the kitchen counter to face him was deliberate. I needed the granite to separate, like a barrier. Because I didn't know if I could stand in front of him again.

Stop all this drama Ryan; he's just some guy you used to fuck.

He's not the first person you dated.

Grow the fuck up.

He sighed placing his hand on his face "All my life, I actually never hoped to meet someone like you."

Cue the unwelcomed warm feeling in my chest. "Oh."

"You're amazing and sweet and kind and perfect. So perfect that it seemed too ridiculous. I thought to myself, Ryan is just too amazing to be true. Something has to fuck this up because my life has never truly been this perfect ever."

Shut UP, I'M NOT PERFECT. DON'T EVER FUCKING CALL ME THAT WORD.

Perfect I am not.

Perfect I am not.

He gave a sad smile.

"And so I did."

Another gulp of burning alcohol and I waited for him to continue. "When you told me what you did before, something just snapped inside me. It's like in that moment I was given a perfect reason why we couldn't be together. Like it was all summed up."

I wanted to talk, to say something. But my lips were shut, they couldn't move. I couldn't find a single way to pry them open.

"I-I'm not stupid." Jason said wearily. "I see how you carry yourself. Some-times when we're walking down the street together I feel a little embar-rassed next to you when you're fully decked out in your expensive stuff and my entire outfit is the price of one fucking shoe. I hate the way I feel when you grab the bills sometimes when we go out and say you've got it when you know I'm a little short because I didn't get to do many gigs during the week. Or even when you buying me groceries because you've noticed that my fridge is empty. It makes me feel sick, useless in fact when it seems like I'm leeching off you and that's the last thing I want to do."

"You're not." I said feeling wobbly. The drinks may have kicked in earlier than expected. "I don't mind doing all those things for you Jason because I care about you. To me it doesn't even matter at all." It surprised me that I hadn't noticed this in Jason. For all my powers of observation didn't pick up on the fact that my boyfriend had been struggling with insecurity.

Guess certain things did escape me.

"But I do." He replied with the same solemn expression "I mind, because as much as I want to accept all your help, I can't. Maybe I'm too proud or a bit arrogant but I can't stand to think that I'm only taking from you and not giving anything in return."

Jason wasn't proud or arrogant. He was kind and considerate. It wasn't his fault that he wasn't automatically sent to receive from everyone who came his way. That was something to be viewed as a noble quality.

"But you were giving me so much." I protested walking away from the kitchen counter to stand directly in front of him. "Jason you made me happy. You made me laugh and feel good about myself and-"

I held myself there. I didn't know how to tell him that he was my first real relationship. The first time I'd dated someone without any ulterior motives or thoughts of using until I got bored.

He looked expectantly "And what Ryan?"

I hesitated "I just really liked you. I still like you. A lot in fact."

Jason didn't say anything. He looked almost emotionless, it seemed like he'd just given up. As if he didn't know what else to say.

It made me feel afraid.

"Ryan, I have feelings for you too but I don't expect you to take me back after what I did and how I ended things with you so abruptly. I let my deeply ridden insecurities cloud my judgment and ended up hurting you in the way I never anticipated before." Jason continued. He stopped to shake his head a little "To be honest I wouldn't take me back if I were you."

This was it.

He was ending things.

He was fully letting me go.

This is it, my mind whispered wickedly to me.

"But apart from being proud, apparently I'm selfish too." He surprised me with a soft smile. Jason nervously played with his fingers "I'm selfish because as much as I should let you go and move on to someone better than me, I can't. I want to be with you too much. It's quite conflicting; wanting someone you shouldn't. I want you Ryan, I need you."

If my eyes were filled with tears at this point, then it was best to blame the alcohol. My chest was constricted, I couldn't breathe. I needed to breathe out. I needed to scream. Lord knows I needed to do something to release all this air trapped inside me.

"You need me." I repeated after him.

"Like I need fucking air. These past few days I haven't been able to stop thinking about you. I wanted to call you but each time my fingers hovered over your number I couldn't dial it because I was so scared and so afraid of what to say to you. How the hell do you start a conversation after hurting someone the way I hurt you?!" Jason asked.

In a bold move, I grabbed his hand. "You made a mistake. Everyone makes mistakes. Yes I was hurt by how you acted and all but I understand why you reacted the way you did. I haven't lived the kind of life that many would be proud of."

"You should know that I don't care if you've slept with a hundred men. You're still Ryan to me." He said quite fiercely taking me aback. Jason had quite a way of surprising me with everything he did. It threw me off my feet every single time. I tightened my grip on his hand. He did the same. It overwhelmed me, having him so close after dreaming about it for the past few days.

My head and everything about me seemed to be pumped with just one singular purpose.

Jason.

Jason.

Jason.

His free thumb gently brushed my cheek and I tried my very best not to flinch because I didn't know when his hand had reached my face.

"You don't have to say anything. In fact, it would probably be best if you didn't. That way it wouldn't be a quick reaction to whatever I've just said." Jason spoke gently.

"Ok." I bit my lip as we both held in a weak laugh.

He leaned forward and pressed his lips against mine. It was quick. Barely lasted a second. But it lingered on my lips after he pulled away and said "Whatever you chose, I'm fine with that."

It still remained even after he gave me what I assumed to be one last smile before leaving my apartment. I just stood there in the middle of my apartment, frozen almost solid. I could still feel Jason pressed close to me.

One thing that I forgot to tell Jason was that I was also capable of being selfish. I took what I wanted without consequence. Maybe it ended up hurting others in the process but collateral damage couldn't be avoided. I was cruel and ruthless at times and my past was a wonderful reminder of that. Most times it was easy for me to suppress those tendencies. But in the right situation and with the right amount of pressure, I would release them.

And now was one of those times.

Blindly grabbing my house keys and wallet, I rushed out of my apartment slamming the door on my way out. Peter at the Lobby looked quite confused when he saw me running out of the elevator with ruffled hair and wild eyes singularly focused.

"Anything wrong?" He asked cautiously.

I shook my head grinning wildly "Not at all."

Everyone who saw me was probably scandalized but I didn't care at all. Running out of the building, I whistled for a cab and jumped into the first one that drove up the curb.

"Take me to Soho." I barked out to the driver. In a calmer setting I might have been much more polite but everything was far too hyped up for me to take it easy. It took about 6 more seconds for me to properly state the address for him.

During the ride I wanted to call Astrid but I knew what she would say and I needed to do this without a speck of doubt in my mind.

"Thanks." I said tossing a hundred into the window of the taxi as I ran into Jason's apartment building. I didn't even throw a bitch fit about the stairs like I normally would but was running fast enough to make The Flash utterly jealous.

Panting but still determined, I rushed to the floor where his apartment was and mentally counted until the familiar sign of 6A came into sight. Taking in a deep breath, I knocked on the door.

No answer.

I knocked again.

There was no answer. I was about to do it the third time when I heard lazy footsteps on the other side of the apartment door.

The knob moved. Jason opened the door with nothing but sweatpants and a look of shock on his face. I stood there a bit sweaty and a lot tired, still in the clothes I wore to have dinner with Cornelius earlier.

"Ryan? What are you doing here?" Jason asked.

"You said that you're a selfish guy sometimes." I recalled. "Well I forgot to let you know that I'm also pretty selfish. Whenever I want something I take it and I don't look back. You say that I deserve better but frankly you're what I want. I don't give a shit about getting what I deserve because life is pretty much unfair and doesn't always give us what we truly deserve. For some crazy reason, I met you and I want to have something real with you and unless you want something different, I'm not willing to walk away like a shitty little martyr. I'm here to take what I want and you're what I want Jason."

Jason looked at for so long that I thought he was going to reject me but he just smiled and pulled me into a bone crushing hug that I didn't mind. I hugged him back with all the energy that I could muster.

"Yes, yes I want this too." He murmured.

His lips found mine in a familiar tango and my chest finally let out the release that it was seeking. It was dirty, rough and plain out passionate. Denied for far too long, he devoured me with such vigor that I welcomed, needed even. Even the very thought of pulling away for air annoyed me to the bone.

"I'm sorry-" Jason tried to apologize again but I gave him a sharp look.

"Don't you dare apologize. I want you to carry me back to that apartment and fuck me till I can't remember my own freaking name." I might as well have commanded.

He grinned holding my waist and letting my jump to wrap my legs around him "As you wish."

The next two hours were an intense blur of scattered clothing, thrusts and moans. Having Jason's body against mine sent chills around every part of my body. With his filthy words whispered right into my ears and my fingers digging painfully into his back, sex had never been so good. Each time with Jason was equally amazing but this had reached a new level yet unexplored. Something primal and animalistic.

The force with which his hips rammed against mine, back arched and mouths in an O shape. Now I understood what all those poets who spoke too much on the subject were raving on about. There was certainly something unbelievable about two bodies uniting the way ours did. Something aesthetic.

"Will you stay?" Jason asked afterwards when we had worn each other out and rest was the only option if we didn't want to break down completely.

He tried to play it off as nonchalance but the underlying vulnerability was present there. I smiled against his chest intertwining our hands together. I wanted him to hold me all the days of my life.

Astrid might have laughed at how disgusting I sounded but the Brooklyn Bridge could have fallen at this point and I wouldn't care.

"Yes. Someone has to make you a decent breakfast after all." I teased.

Jason rolled his eyes but smile nevertheless "I'm glad. I missed you."

"I missed you too." I said with a yawn. Later he said when he thought I was sleeping, something that made my entire body freeze and I surely didn't have an answer to. Something that made me feel fear like never before.

"I love you Ryan."

Raise your hands up if you were expecting that ending.

Chapter 20

- -

Wow another update in less than 24 hours I am so freaking awesome and you all should bow to me. Lol. Just joking. Hope you like it though.

SONG - ROSE GOLD - PENTATONIX

It was an alarm that woke me up. Jason's alarm to be precise because I would never voluntarily set up an alarm to wake up from sleep. Like no fucking way. Jason had a thing about waking up at the same time each day because it helped you stay alert or something. The memory made me smile and I was grateful for the first time about hearing that familiar dreaded alarm clock.

My head settled against the warm chest I was lying on and for a moment, it seemed quite easy to forget all about the stupid alarm clock.

A too cheerful ray of light was already peeking from the closed curtains in the bedroom. That meant that it was probably past the time to get up but my body was far too delightfully worn and sore to do so. It was Friday and I had one class but with my current situation it seemed more likely that I would skip rather than attend.

Jason stirred underneath me. I stiffened my body so that he wouldn't wake up. Luckily, he was a pretty light sleeper and it served the situation perfectly. He snored softly so I assumed that he had gone back to sleep.

"Jason." I called softly.

No answer. He was definitely asleep. Gently peeling my body away from his, I straddled his body until I climbed off the bed completely and my bare feet were cushioned against the plush carpet. A lone boxer hung off the bed post and I wore it to cover my nudity.

I glanced at Jason's sleeping body one more time before leaving the bedroom to his quaint kitchen. Clean and scrubbed as I'd last seen it.

Didn't even realize when an unconscious smile seeped in.

My iPhone was placed next to one of the pots and I figured that during our frantic rendezvous, I must have thrown it there. Thankfully there was no damage at all, just a lot of missed calls and text messages. Some from Astrid and Jay mainly asking about how the date went and if I would see Cornelius again.

Cornelius.

My stomach dropped when I finally remembered him. I'd been so caught up with reconciling with Jason that I'd forgotten all about him and where he stood with me. The poor man was probably off thinking that we had something together and breaking that bubble was going to be a cruel thing to do.

There was no way I was going to lead him on so the solution was to tell him that I couldn't let it go on further between us now that Jason had come back. Or at least he had come back and it seemed like he was going to stay.

I love you Ryan.

Everything about me was sore and I didn't want to waste time pondering on things which would surely upset me. Right now it was time to enjoy the moment and hope that it would last long enough. We definitely needed this.

"Ryan?" I heard Jason's faint voice from the bedroom.

"In here!" I shouted in reply as I picked out a couple of bowls and a frying pan from his cupboard. Picking up a bag of flour, I listened until his footsteps came closer to the kitchen.

"Morning." Jason said with a hint of his always shy smile.

I couldn't help myself. I left the mix I was turning and walked over to kiss him. His lips were warm and inviting. My hands placed over his shoulders and pushed our bodies even closer. It felt far too wonderful to be true. I must have been dreaming. But even dreams didn't feel this good.

"Morning." I whispered after we pulled away. "You ok?"

He nodded hesitantly "Yeah. For a moment when I woke up, I thought you'd left."

His words pained me. He was still so shaken that he thought I would leave him. Firmly placing my hand on his cheek, I looked at Jason right in the eye "I'm not leaving you. Not unless you want me to."

His mouth twitched with a smile "I'm glad."

Now it was my turn to smile "Good. I was busy making you breakfast."

"Ah now you've got me all excited." Jason said following me to the messy kitchen counter. "I'm always excited when you cook."

I snorted "Then you should thank all the recipe books I read after meeting you."

Shivers went through me when a kiss was placed on my shoulder "Thank you." I gripped the wooden spoon tighter because if not I might have said "Fuck the food" and jumped on Jason instead. However, we needed to eat and to also resolve some certain things and although sex was good, it would definitely distract us.

"I love cooking now." I said absently. "In the past I hated it but now not so much."

"My good influence." Jason said with a wink sitting down on the sofa opposite me. Rolling my eyes playfully, I continued mixing the pancake batter. There was silence. Comforting silence were we both acknowledged each other's presence well enough but there was nothing else that needed to be said. Just knowing that Jason was there seemed good enough for me.

It wasn't until after the food was ready and we were both eating on the kitchen counter that I finally said something. Dropping the fork, I faced Jason holding an extreme measure of seriousness on my face.

"I need to say something."

He chewed slowly "Anything."

I took in a deep breath "I-I, don't want us to lie to each other. I might not be able to tell you everything on my mind but I don't want any lies between us. Lies complicate and tear things apart. If we're going to give this a chance then there should be no lies."

He nodded. "Understood."

"Good. And I want you to know that I've never been in a real relationship before. I'm not perfect and I'm definitely going to make some mistakes but I want you to know that I'm going to try my best to get this right. I want to get this right." I said with shaky determination.

"Thank you." Jason answered quietly. His hand found mine in a comforting gesture "There are so many questions that I want to ask. But as you said you're not ready to say everything yet and I'm not going to ask them until you're ready."

"Ok." I thanked him.

"For the record on my path, I'm going to do everything to make sure that I don't fuck this up." he bit his lip looking a bit hesitant "I'm going to stop feeling sorry for myself. Even though they feel a bit unreachable at times, I won't give up on my dreams. I'll work as hard as I can and I'm sure I'll be able to make it."

His conviction made me made me feel pleased deep down inside.

"You'll accept help when you need it." I added.

Jason nodded with a faint smile "Yeah. I'll try my best to hold in my pride when it's necessary. I just don't want to end up losing you again."

"You won't." I assured. This time would be different. We both knew that things were going to be as easy as they were previously but Jason and I were willing to try. We were both terribly selfish people unfortunately.

He kissed our intertwined hands making me smile again. Gosh I was turning into such a sappy little fucker. My nineteen year old self must be watching in utter disgust.

"I was on a date last night when you came." I confessed since I had been the one to come up with the whole honesty policy thing. That didn't mean that I wasn't worried Jason would be extremely unhappy since going with all relationship protocol, it was probably too soon after we broke up.

Jason tensed a little but remained relatively calm "Oh. Did you plan on seeing him again?"

"Not after you came to apologize. He's a nice guy but I don't have as much interest in him as he does in me it seems.

The tenseness left him and was replaced with visible relief "Guess I came just in time then."

"Yeah." I said wistfully. "I was going to let him know later that I don't want us to pursue it further."

He nodded enthusiastically "Yes please." I had to keep from laughing at his eagerness. He was truly an overgrown puppy.

Just watching Jason smile made me feel that we would and could definitely make this work. I for one was ready for it. Utterly and completely.

While enjoying my breakfast with my newly reinstated boyfriend, I was reminded of what that asshole ex of mine Jon had said in the grocery store.

He was wrong; people did change for the better.

"Thanks for meeting up with me." I stated with a nervous and grateful smile all packed in one. Cornelius comfortably sat opposite me. "No problem."

We were at a random coffee shop I told him to meet me at earlier in the day. Jason had encouraged me to do this only if I wanted to but I still couldn't push away multiple scenarios about how wrong this could go in my head.

"Something you wanted to say?" He asked.

I played with the rim of my Styrofoam coffee "I had a great time last night and you're a wonderful man but-"

He raised a hand to signal stop which confused me immensely "You don't want to take this any further do you?"

How incredibly perceptive of him to figure this out. It made this easier and harder at the same time. At least I tried to look apologetic "I'm really sorry. You're a wonderful man but, but I've already met someone who for some reason I can't seem to let go of."

"Do they feel the same way?" He asked in a quieter tone than I had anticipated. Did Jason feel the same way?

I love you Ryan.

"He does." I replied not looking up to face the man seated opposite me. "Somehow the way we both arrived at that conclusion wasn't the best but he does. I just don't think it would be fair for me to lead you along."

Cornelius gave a brave face and nodded "I understand. I can't lie and say I'm not disappointed because I definitely saw the two of us going places but maybe it's better this way. I truly and honestly wish you happiness all the love in the world Ryan. I just feel a bit sad that it's not with me."

"Thank you." I expressed in relief. "You are a truly wonderful guy Cornelius and I hope there's someone who really deserves you out there."

"I hope so too." He replied with a faint smile. I stood up and gave him one last hug before pulling away. "And to be sincere, I hope that he truly deserves everything you gave to give him Ryan."

Instead of answering, I just smiled and walked away to hail a cab. If only he really knew.

I love you Ryan.

If only he really knew that it felt like I was the one who didn't feel like I deserved everything Jason had to give me.

You guys like this story right? Just checking.

So Ry and Jason seem back together but fear not! Drama is on the way because I'm a grade A bitch who can't leave these two in peace. (^_^) oh well.

Chapter 21 (Greendale)

Early update *gets standing ovation*

SONG - MONSTER - EMINEM FT RIHANNA

"How's LA been?" I asked with a pleasant smile on my face as I walked to the coffee shop. School had ended an hour ago and I wanted to get something before heading home. Chris was home and I needed time to avoid since he'd gotten all up in my business more often lately.

"Sunny and sizzling." She sang out making me laugh. Even after all this time it was hard to think that I could be friends with someone like Astrid. She was elegant and classy, miles away from my lane. But she told me that with time I'd be able to ease into a room oozing the same confidence she did.

So far it had been working.

"I'm thinking of making a detour to somewhere warm and tropical during Christmas break. Do you want to join me?" She asked.

I bit my lip, it was a very tempting offer "It'll be Christmas by then and I don't think my family will want me to go away."

Well my Dad to be honest. I didn't care what Chris and (most times my Mom) thought about whatever I did with my life.

The smell of cinnamon buns and vanilla wafted through my nostrils inviting me to come in further.

"Well let me know if you'll change your mind. Toddles." She greeted in a deliberately preppy voice to make me laugh.

"Bye." I said not even helping my chuckles.

Sam the barista already knew my order since I had the same thing every single day. I asked him to add two cinnamon buns for a little spice then went to sit on a table next to the window to enjoy my treats.

With nothing else to do I decided to kill time by doing my homework. Astrid told me that just because I'd gotten a makeover didn't meant that I had to neglect my schoolwork. Pretty people can only go so far in life, she said, but pretty people who are smart end up taking over the world. Of course I already knew that fact well but it was nice to know that she cared about that aspect of my life too.

"You've been avoiding me." Gerard's voice snapped my attention.

"You don't understand." I said. I hadn't even noticed when he came in and made his way to my table. For the past few weeks I'd done a successful job of dodging him around the town. It was all for a particular purpose but he'd managed to find me earlier than I expected so I now had to improvise.

"Then make me understand." He persuaded further. "Make me understand why you've been avoiding me all this time."

I sighed dramatically "Look. My parents were asking questions about where I was. I got grounded and lost my phone privileges."

The look on Gerard' face softened exactly the way I wanted it to.

"I'm sorry." He said genuinely. "Didn't mean to get you into trouble."

"It's ok." I assured him. "They're strict but I managed to sneak away plenty of times. I'll come see you at our usual place during the week."

"I'm just glad that it wasn't out of your own free will." He looked visibly relieved. The coffee shop was a bit deserted today so only the barista and some woman typing furiously on her laptop remained.

"But what about today?" Gerard asked desperately. "Why can't we see today?"

Today I'd ditched Government class for a quick romp with Emmett in the janitor's closet. He was particularly affectionate and not rough at all when he cradled my waist as he held me up to fuck. It was good; the feeling of having power over someone and knowing that you could bend them under your control at will felt so freaking good.

"I have an errand to run for my Mom." I lied easily. He nodded, he understood. Family always came first right?

"Tomorrow." He said.

"Tomorrow." I confirmed.

"I wish I could kiss you right now." He whispered between us. Of course he couldn't keeping appearances was practically the mantra of his family.

"Keep all your kisses for tomorrow my love." I said flirtatiously. He grinned "Of course."

Shortly after Gerard left, I got a text from Emmett saying that we should meet up in the abandoned park downtown. Sometimes he liked to request that we met in strange places in case of prying eyes but I was far too tired already.

Can't.

My reply was simple.

My phone pinged again after two literal seconds.

Please. It's super important for our project.

The cryptic way he typed meant that he probably didn't want anyone to know where he was going if asked. I didn't want to go but he would keep bugging me and avoiding him wouldn't be quite as easy since we both went to the same school.

With a sigh and complete disregard for common sense, I hopped into my car and drove off to the abandoned park. Part of me hoped that he wasn't planning on fucking me against a tree trunk or something. I didn't need to drive home plucking pieces of wood from my ass.

I arrived scanning around the area for his familiar blue Tundra. I parked my car walking around hoping that Emmett didn't lead me on some stupid wild goose chase because I really didn't need any of that at the moment.

"Emmett." I called out close the dirty pond.

"He's not here." Was the reply I received which sent my heart pounding harder than ever. It was Nathan Coffey behind me with no sign of his annoyingly horny best friend in sight. Just the two of us. I shifted away subtly, not wanting to give away the fact I was scared of being alone with him.

"Why did he text me then?" I asked.

"He didn't. I did." Nathan replied easily. He produced Emmett's silver iPhone from his pocket and waved it a little "He's at my house playing Halo. Gets pretty into the game that he loses all focus. It's so easy to take stuff from him then."

The son of a bitch tricked me.

"What do you want?" I asked carefully.

He shrugged "I want you to stop what you're doing."

"What?" did he know that was seeing both his brother and his best friend? The thought scared me more than ever. I didn't want my plans to go awry this way.

"You think I don't know that it's a coincidence that you got paired up with Emmett? And what, after you come from your little make over? I'm not an idiot. Stop everything you've been doing to get my attention Ryan." He said steadily.

Amazing.

This guy really did think the world revolved around him didn't he?

I laughed "Seriously? I'm busy living my life and you think it's some ploy to get you to notice me? Unbelievable. Perhaps the years you spent making my life a living hell wasn't enough so I decided to go through all this trouble for you to do it for me again. Get over yourself."

Nathan fumed "Shut up faggot." He was angry now. Maybe I'd egged him on a little too much. But he only moved closer towards me "Isn't it enough? All these years you made me want you, to want you in the worst way ever. I'm not gay but you just had to keep tempting me didn't you?"

And that was when it was all handed to me on a silver platter. So the reason Nathan Coffey had spent years of my life pushing me down, beating me, and breaking my spirit was because he was trying to fight his attraction towards me?

It was all too much but it made sense.

"I didn't do anything to you." I defended. "Whatever you felt is natural-"

"Shut up!" He screamed grabbing my shirt with his fist. The scene was all too familiar. He was going to punch my face in and leave me with bruises to count. He would again remind me how worthless I am.

"I have a great life! A hot girlfriend and I'm king of the football field! You're not going to ruin it with your stupid little distractions ok?! Because I'm not gay." He kept on saying.

"Ok." I replied weakly wanting him to let me go.

But Nathan didn't. Instead he decided to forcefully pull me into the most disturbing kiss of my life. In the kiss I felt all the hatred, the confliction and the desire all at once. What a fable it must be to get addicted to something you hate.

"If you tell anyone about this, I'll fucking kill you." He hissed before letting go of my shirt and leaving me alone and bewildered in the park.

My bully had an obsession with me. He hated but wanted me at the same time. How ironic. Except that I couldn't feel bad for him one bit. In fact, my hatred grew. So he decided to ruin my life because he couldn't get his together? Right on the money then. I would ruin his life in equal piece.

His little confession just made it a little sweeter for me to take my revenge.

someone tell me if this was shit or not. I need to know because I just wrote this entire chapter half-asleep and am beyond caring right now.

Chapter 22

I know this is short but someone distracted while writing this...........st op thinking so dirty ;)

The gif above because we all need a bit of Jay to keep the day bright.

"I hope that you know what you're doing." Jay said seriously. We were currently having lunch at our usual diner since my class was cancelled and I was going to work in about two hours. After I told him about making up with Jason he'd been supportive but more warnings that insults were spoken towards the end.

"I do know what I'm doing." I replied sorting through my basket of fries. "He might have taken it a bit hard in the beginning but we're doing better now."

Our relationship had pretty much picked up from where we left it but with a few minor adjustments to add. Jason didn't seem as reserved as he previously was. He talked more openly even though he seemed hesitant to say some things. But it was ok by me.

Still I barely shared anything on my side and it left me with a tingling sensation of guilt. We both promised to be honest with each other but I had been leaving certain things out. It wasn't lying; they just never came up as real issues and for now I was grateful.

It didn't feel like I was ready enough to explain to Jason why I ate more some days and less on the others.

"I know but I just want you to be careful Ryan." Jay repeated.

"Hey, you're the one who always said that a real relationship would be better than what I was doing." I defended. "I enjoyed my time playing around but I like being with Jason more. He grounds me."

"That's great but not what I was - never mind." He seemed distracted.

"Anything wrong?" I asked cautiously because it wasn't a new occurrence. Jay had been a little distant and less jovial for the past few days. He was great at deflecting each time I asked but now the issue seemed big enough that he ignored his favorite lunch.

And nothing could normally distract Jay from his fries and onion rings.

He shook his head "It's me and Patrick. Things have been a bit difficult lately. He's been sleeping in the guest room for a week now."

That sparked my interest. It would be an understatement to say that I was surprised at his words. Patrick and Jay were pretty much the equivalent of a Disney couple. Sickening amounts of fluff radiated from them. Yes they obviously were expected to have disagreements but it was mostly about small, insignificant things.

Certainly nothing that would warrant Patrick sleeping on the couch for a week.

"Wanna talk about it?" I enquired.

He shrugged tiredly "My parents called me about a month ago."

That I did not know. The impression I'd always gotten was that Jay's family had treated him as though he was dead ever since he told them of his relationship with Patrick. Jay told me that his parents were conservative to the core and didn't take even hesitate before sending him out on the street. Only his kind grandmother made sure that he had a large share in her will before she died so that he wasn't completely defenseless in the world.

"About what?"

"They said that they wanted to see me. They said that they understood the gravity of their error and were willing to accept me for who I am." Jay said absently playing with a fry.

"So what was the problem?" I asked leaning back against the booth.

He let out a puff of air "Patrick didn't want me to. He said that if they were sincere then they'd seek me out instead of making me go to them. He said that they hadn't communicated to me in about 3 years and they expected me to just drop everything and come meet them."

"You two fought." I stated.

He nodded "Terribly. We've never fought the way we did before. I accused him of being jealous and wanting to keep me all to himself. It was unfair and terrible of me to say. He's always been supportive of me but yet I just threw it all in his face like he was some controlling fiend."

By how I noticed how shaky his voice was becoming and how close to tears he was. I placed my hand on his for comfort. He gave me a grateful look.

"The worst part was that when I drove up to meet them, I found out that the only reason they wanted us to talk was because one of my Dad's stupid business associates has a gay son and they thought that some sort of archaic matchmaking thing could be arranged. I felt so stupid. Patrick was right and now I can't even face him because of how stupid I feel. He was just trying to warn and protect me yet I acted like a downright bitch." He concluded.

My hold on him tightened "I don't think he hates you or anything. Patrick is most likely hurt but I'm sure if the two of you talk it out it'll get better."

"It's just that I said some really mean things. Things I don't mean but obviously he doesn't know that now." Jay sniffled.

Seeing him this way made me feel bad.

Jay was always the epitome of sass and happiness. Seeing him as anything but wasn't a pretty sight to behold.

"Then that just means you have to show him how sincere you really are." I advised. "Patrick cares about you intensely and I doubt that he's going to leave you because of this. But right now it's your responsibility to take the reins on this and apologize first."

Jay sniffed again "Goodness when did you get to great with relationship advice?"

I couldn't even hide my smile even if I tried "Dunno. Luck." The characteristics of being in one had started to rub on me.

He used one of the napkins to wipe his barely there tears "Keep it up. I like this new Ryan. I liked the old one just fine but you're a lot more emotionally open now."

"What? Was I too much of a heartless bitch before?" I asked sarcastically.

He laughed "Shut up and buy me dessert."

"You shouldn't have dessert in the afternoon. It's bad for your figure." I mocked already signaling the waiter to order some chocolate cake because that was Jay's favorite.

He was unimpressed "I've just had an emotional moment and I demand confectionaries. Now be a good boy and get me some."

Ordinarily I might have decked him for saying that but I was in a good mood so I'd let it go.

For now.

\-

"I love payday." My co-worker Marissa said dramatically holding her envelope to her chest as we both walked out of the store. I rolled my eyes but gave a smile "Yep. Almost makes the job feel worth it."

"Tell me about it." She scoffed. "If I have to explain the difference between silk and satin one more time to some 14 year old with a credit card, I'm going to spontaneously combust."

"Exaggeration but I get your point." I said with a nod. "Are you going home straight?"

She sighed wearing her scarf over her neck "Yeah gotta pick my kid from my Mom's house. I just want to cuddle up with my little man and forget about all the worries in the world."

Marissa had a five year old son from her former fiancé. She said that they were going to get married until his family poisoned his brain into thinking that she was a fortune climber. I felt bad for her because knowing Marissa; she was the exact opposite of that. Just because she grew up humbly in the South and came to New York for a better job didn't mean that she was hunting for money. People like her were miles away from people like me on the morality scale. On the good side.

Long story short, she left him, had a kid and refuses to acknowledge his existence. When I asked her if he knew about his son she replied no and that she wasn't going to tell him because she didn't want her child growing up in such a toxic environment.

"I don't want my son facing judgment from people saying that his mother only had him to trap his father. Teddy is far better than that and if I have to work to take care of him, I will." she had said.

It was something that I wasn't familiar with but respected at the same time.

"Good night Marissa. See you on Tuesday." I waved as she went in the direction of the subway.

"Bye Ryan." She smiled before turning away.

I was a little tired but more than willing to walk just so that I could get home to Jason. My whole body thrummed with excitement at the thought of seeing him.

He was meeting me at my apartment since we were at his previously and he had a meeting the next day quite close to the area.

But by the time I got to my apartment building, I was in for a surprise.

Because standing right outside, was my brother Chris in the flesh.

Dun, Dun, Dun.....

I've been craving fanart. If you have any don't hesitate to send it.

Chapter 23

Might contain some pretty triggering stuff at the end.

SONG - HOUSE ON FIRE - SIA

He looked different.

Older.

I don't know why it surprised me to see lanky brother now a bit solider and leanly muscled. His chestnut hair was fuller and wavier. He looked a little taller, almost the same height as I was. I guess all these changes shouldn't have been so surprising to me considering I hadn't seen him in nearly four years.

"How did you find this place?" My voice was sharp and paranoid. I didn't tell any of my family members where I lived in the city apart from Dad. And I was forced to do so since he had to send a few letters and checks to me. None of them had ever visited at my insistence. With the brash and wild way I'd been living, it was better that way.

Chris stuffed his hands into his pockets "Hi Ryan."

"Don't leave my question unanswered." I snapped.

His eyes widened in surprise. As though he hadn't expected me to sound this way "Dad leaves his stuff scattered around the kitchen sometimes. He left a few mails and I took a look."

Made perfect sense.

"What are you doing here? How did you get to New York?" those were the next round of questions fired at him.

Chris bunched his lips together "I'm in the Art club at school and so we took a trip to see the Met and some other galleries. Figured that I'd take the time to also see you."

"Really?" my tone hardened.

"Yes. I have the phone number of the accompanying teachers and a note signed by our parents to say that I could go." He stated confidently. It was proof that I should believe him.

I processed the information "Why?"

"Because I have so many things I want to say to you. Perhaps things that I should have said a long time ago but for one reason and many I didn't." his tone was sullen. "It's more likely right now that you're going to call Mom and Dad to have my ass shipped back to Greendale ASAP. But I hope that maybe you'll be interested in what I have to say now."

I was conflicted.

A very large part of me did want to call my parents and kick him out of my sight. It was perfectly rational after all; my little brother who I'd hated for part of my life shows out of the blue and wants to talk. I should be mad. I should be furious. I should screech at the top of my voice that I never wanted to see him again.

But a little, weaker part of me was painfully curious about what Chris wanted to say. I knew my brother and he wasn't a risk taker. He wouldn't risk bunking on a clearly not well monitored school trip for a cause he didn't see as important.

But just because it was important to him didn't mean that it was the same to me. There was no obligation for me to care. I weighed my options and the most unlikely part won out.

"Come on." I walked past him into the building. I didn't know what I was doing and honestly it seemed best not to think about it.

Surprised, Chris quickly followed after me. His Conversed squeaked on the marble floors with each hurrying step he took after me. Pete looked up from his desk with a small frown which transformed into brief surprise at the sight of my brother trailing behind. I gave him a small nod indicating that I wasn't in the mood for small talk this evening and he reciprocated it.

In the elevator, my brother's labored breathing was loud. I stood in front of him mostly because I didn't want a reason for our eyes to dart in the same direction. He was obviously awestruck and mentally appraising his new environment the way I had done when I first entered here. The visible gaucherie that enveloped me, reaffirming that this was now my home. It was wonderfully terrifying.

But I forced myself to look away because I didn't want to compare how similar our expressions probably were.

The elevator reached my floor and I didn't waste any time walking to my apartment door and opening it.

"Nice place." Chris said casually. In a moment I expected him to ask how I could afford it.

My reply would be something akin to telling him to shut up.

"How long do you have?" I asked instead going to the fridge to grab a few drinks. He checked his phone "About two hours. Keller and Donnie are going to cover for me but the teachers usually inspect by 9 pm so I'm good until then."

It was currently 6:57 pm.

"Do you drink now?" I questioned holding two bottles of beer. He eyed them for a moment "A few times during parties."

"Good." I tossed him one which he skillfully caught. After coming to silent terms with the fact that I had knowingly given my 17 year old brother beer, I moved over to the couch and plopped myself on it.

"Talk now."

Chris's expression softened now "I'm sorry."

I leaned closer not quite sure I'd heard right "What?"

"I said I'm sorry." His voice was louder now. My fists clenched tighter against the can of beer "Is that so?"

"Yes." My brother looked down. "All those things I did to you were wrong and uncalled for. I'm sorry for everything."

There was silence in the entire apartment at his confession. My cold fingers tapped against the throw pillows seeping some warmth into them. The bright twinkly lights that represented the city enthusiastically poured themselves into the living room courtesy of the floor to ceiling windows. For a moment I contemplated installing curtains to block the lights. There was too much light in the moment.

"You're sorry." I echoed.

Next thing, Chris jerked in surprise at my hysterical laugher, eyes shot up in disbelief at my actions. I laughed so hard that my beer nearly spilled over on the Persian rug if it wasn't for the fact that I was clutching it tightly.

"What's so funny?" He asked in obvious confusion.

I smiled "You little brother. 'I'm sorry for everything.' It's funny the way you say those words like they're supposed to fix everything. As an 'I'm sorry' will change all that's happened. You're really fucking hilarious Chris."

His face hardened "What am I supposed to do?"

My smile turned bitter "You're supposed to go back in time to stop all of this from happening but you're a little short on ability so I guess we can't get all we want can we?"

"Ryan-"

I raised a hand up to stop him. A clear sign of authority, silencing him for the time being. A move that surprised even me. I was used to power plays with too many people to care but not once in my life had I ever pulled such a move on my brother.

While my surprise was carefully masked, Chris made no show of hiding his.

"You tormented me for years, called me names, and broke me to the fucking ground till there was nothing left of me but dust and pain. I wanted to kill myself." My tone grew colder at each point I made. "And all you can fucking say is sorry?"

He swallowed painfully. "I know it must be terribly hard for you to believe me Ryan but I'm sorry."

"Please just stop saying sorry." I groaned massaging my temples "That word is giving me a serious headache at this rate. Dearest brother if it were up to me I'd never want to see you in my life ever again. In fact from the moment I left town you became dead to me. I don't have a brother."

Each word I spoke visibly tore Chris down but I swallowed the guilt and let urge to hurt overwhelm me. I wanted him to feel it just the way I'd felt every word, every slur and insult from his mouth.

"Ever since you left I've tried to apologize to you, to make you understand how terrible I feel about myself for making you feel this way." He pleaded.

I snorted standing up from the couch "Of course that's why."

"What's why?"

"The only reason you came to apologize is because your little conscience seems to be beating you up. Somehow you got struck with feelings and now you want to shake them off you as quickly as possible." I dropped the barely sipped beer on the kitchen granite.

"That's not it." Chris defended shooting up from the couch.

"Then why? Why now did you choose to say this to me now?" I moved closer to him with a challenging tone. His eyes were clouded and coated with so many things I couldn't make out. For a brief moment, sudden grief hit me. This was my little brother. We had grown up together happily. We actually loved each other once. We built snowmen and sandcastles together. We shared ice cream sundaes and chocolate bars with eager smiles.

His bright innocent features once shone with pride at me. And mine reflected back the same way.

Now he was here – all grown up. Bundled with demons and secrets of his own. Ones that I would never truly know.

"Because now I understand how you felt all those years and everything that I did to you. I understand how bad it was." His voice was hollow as he spoke. "I understood ever since you left town and moved here. Each time I wanted to tell you this but you rejected and wouldn't take my calls. I understand though, I wouldn't want to talk to me either."

It was my turn to swallow now. "I honestly don't know what to say or feel Chris." It was the first time I'd spoken his name out loud. My mouth was heavy with familiarity. It felt so natural.

"That's ok." My brother responded quietly.

I leaned against the counter suddenly feeling weak "In a million years I didn't think that this would ever happen. That I would ever want to see you again." There was a spark of hope I could see. He wanted to hope that I would let it go. That we could move past this. Somehow, I wanted that too. Years of carrying anger and hatred were more burdening than anyone could imagine. What a relief it would be to just throw it all away and be free for once.

"Do you forgive me Ryan? I'd understand if you don't." Chris's voice was quiet. Afraid. Hopeful. Sad. It made me want to envelope him in a hug and announce that everything was ok.

But alas, nothing was every truly that easy.

"I don't know." I answered honestly.

His face fell dejectedly. There was no more hope. No more reason to in fact. His risk was all for nothing. He had failed.

My heart burst on the inside.

"Thank you for being honest." He said with a bitter smile. "It's actually refreshing."

"Ok." I didn't know what else to say. "Where are you staying?"

"Some hotel down at Bushwick. Fucking sucks though." Chris wiped his forehead. Didn't bother telling him that Bushwick sucked in general.

"Quite a trip." I noted.

He shrugged "I took a cab."

Instinctively I dug into my pocket and brought out a hundred dollar bill "Here for the cab back." This was far too much for the cab though. He looked as though he wanted to say no but collected it with mumbled thanks. I was glad that he didn't say no.

"I'll let myself go down." Chris said. "Goodbye Ryan. I don't think you want me to see you again, even if I wanted to."

"Bye." I mumbled watching my brother let himself out of the apartment while I just stood there. Five minutes past and I noticed my face was wet. Tears were falling and I didn't even acknowledge them until now. The truth was that I didn't know if I could forgive my brother ever, if there would be a chance for me to just offload all the remnants of my past forever. If it could ever truly be that simple.

Without warning I rushed to the bathroom and jammed my fingers down my throat until I vomited my lunch from a few hours before. After doing so I laid on the floor crying and hiccupping without a single care.

It was where I remained until Jason came and found me.

There were some tears right there.

Comments?

Part 2

T O PUT THE PAST BEHIND YOU, YOU MUST ACCEPT
THAT YOU'VE MOVED BEYOND IT

Ruth (Hell on Wheels)

Chapter 24

"Would you like some cookies?" Astrid offered. I shook my head patting my stomach "Ate a big lunch." What a lie. My stomach was growling in fury. I didn't eat anything but toast and hot chocolate for breakfast after Jason had practically forced it on me. She eyed me suspiciously "Sure? They're fresh from the oven. I even added those ridiculous sprinkles you like so much." The offer was quite tempting but I couldn't. My body craved it but my mind refused. I'd learned a long time ago that my emotions had a large impact on my appetite.

My fist clenched "Maybe later."

She dropped it haphazardly on the table "If you say so. I was just being a good friend and giving you some study snacks."

Despite my irritation, I smiled "Thanks."

Astrid watched me "You know, when you called me saying that you wanted to come over and study, I didn't really think you actually meant study. I thought it was a new code for gossiping about hot boys asses."

I snorted a laugh "Does it surprise you that I actually take my education seriously? My GPA is 3.24 you know."

She sighed dropping her hands on the white and gold glass dining table "I'd be quite disappointed if you didn't. Education is important. No one wants to marry an illiterate."

"Ha, I never thought of that." I said dryly.

"Hmm. Lord knows that my Father nearly dragged by the hair when I refused to go to university." Astrid stated casually examining her cuticles.

"Really?" I enquired fiddling with my pen.

"Yes. It was either that or to join the army which my mom wouldn't even dream of letting me." She replied. "So I ended up earning a double degree in Political Science and Economics from The University of Copenhagen. Useless, since there's actually no realistic reason for me to use it since I'm not going into politics. I don't even want to. It's a certificate attached to my name so that I seemed educated and therefore more desirable to anyone who approaches me. Amusing really. Why does four years of wasting away at some school prove that I'm worth something? I should be either way."

"Didn't know you saw it that way." I observed.

She shrugged "Doesn't matter. I paid my dues to my family. Now they let me live my life the way I want to." It was rare for Astrid to talk about herself this way. She was careful; she didn't let anything that hinted about her paternal side slip. Her Mom was an open subject, they were quite close from what I'd seen and didn't care to hide the fact. Her father was a different story though.

All I knew was that he and her mother had divorced and it ended there. Astrid kept her Dad and every issue concerning him on the other side of the Atlantic any time she came into the country. The two separate worlds were not dragged together. Sometimes I think the reason she liked coming to America so much was the mild anonymity. Denmark wasn't like England. Very few people actually knew that they practiced monarchy over there.

In crude terms, they weren't popular and no one outside of their country plus allies really gave a shit about them. Very much to her delight.

"Didn't know you studied Political Science." I said after a while.

She smiled tightly "Now you do." There was no need to say more. We both knew that the conversation was over.

Once again my eyes returned to my book. I'd been on the same line for the past two minutes now. My mind seemed to be branching into difference locations all at once and it was annoying that I couldn't focus well enough.

Last night I had to lie to Jason that the reason I'd vomited was because I ate some bad shellfish. I wasn't sure if he believed me or not but at least he didn't press forward for an answer. He just made me some tea and tucked me into bed which I as beyond grateful for.

My brother was always a toxic presence in my life.

Whether Chris meant to or not, he always caused me deep anguish whenever he was around. There were times when I was still in high school before I met Astrid that he would walk into a room without saying anything but his eyes spoke volumes. Those were the moments I dreaded more than ever.

It was one thing for someone to verbally say that they hate you. They may not give it away quite easily; at least you can watch them smile and pretend without a clue. But for you to be able to tell just from the look in their eyes, it's a whole another ball game entirely.

Because it takes a deeply serious level of hatred for you to be able to let someone know how you despise them just from your eyes.

That's how my brother let his show.

Four years later, he comes waltzing back into my life with a whole new ideology. How does anyone believe that that sort of hatred just got mysteriously wiped away and forgiveness is in order?

I surely didn't.

Although a part of me wanted it to be that straightforward. But it couldn't be. Life's problems couldn't simply be solved with a sorry. If that was the case, there would be no need for police or the law or punishment.

A murderer would simply apologize and all would be well again.

Sadly my many deaths would not go unpunished that way.

"Ryan!" Astrid shouted startling me.

"Jeez." I jumped in my chair. "What the hell Astrid?"

She had a look of disbelief on her face "What the hell is wrong with you? I've called your name about 4 times and you've been staring at your fucking pen."

Closing my eyes, I sighed "I'm sorry. Just distracted is all."

She leaned back against her chair "Doesn't sound like a simple distraction. Tell me what the problem is. Is it Jason? Is he treating you right?"

"He is. We're great." I assured her. "I saw Chris yesterday." Not many things could surprise Astrid but from the look on her face it, this was one of the few things that did. Her speech faltered "What did he want?"

"Forgiveness." The word was heavy on my lips and painful to my heart.

"Do you think that I should forgive him?"

She was quiet. "I don't know what to say."

I wanted to laugh. Astrid was never short of words. "No words of advice?" I asked her. She hesitated "Ryan, giving you advice is something I'll always strive to do as long as I can. But in all honesty, there are some things you unfortunately have to figure out of yourself. I don't have all the answers."

"I wish you did though." I smiled bitterly. "You're like my fairy godmother. You swished a wand and changed my life."

"Sometimes I truly wonder if it was for the better." Astrid immediately cut in. In that moment I wanted to get angry at her words but I couldn't. Her reasoning made sense. As supportive as she'd always been on my lifestyle choices, there was a part of her that worried it would lead me further into destruction. I'd wondered that sometimes. Seducing men to give me the life that I'd always wanted had its thrills and perks. But in the long run it won't be that way forever. The world has a way of squeezing out all you have before there's nothing left of you. Even pretty little dolls have a shelf life.

To my relief, it seemed like that was no longer my life.

I had Jason now.

"You saved me." My voice was quiet. "I'll always be grateful for that."

"Saving everyone, until you forget to save yourself." She whispered quietly. Something was going on with her. I didn't know what it was but I would find out.

Astrid was strong. She was the kind of person who didn't bend over to the wind currents. But if something could get how down this way, then I had a real reason to be afraid.

"I feel giddy." I confessed to Jason as we walked across the set. He snorted "I can't see why."

I laughed "Because I'm on the set of a photo shoot."

"It's not a big deal." He shrugged. I stared at my boyfriend like he was a mad man "It's a DIAMANDIS shoot! Vogue wouldn't even get me this hyped."

DIAMANDIS was one of the top fashion magazines to ever grace the world of print media. I had a subscription that wasn't ending any time soon. And now Jason had snatched a job as one of their main paid photographers. I was so proud of him. When he called me to relay the good news, I didn't even wait before rushing to the other side of the city just to give him a congratulations kiss. He blushed like a peach but it was all in good faith.

We went for lunch during his break before Jason offered me a tour.

"I hope this is allowed." I said walking up closer to him.

He nodded "It's cool. Suzy, our boss, is great. A little stiff but she's cool."

"Talking trash about me already?" a female voice interrupted us. Jason immediately went into work mode. "Oh I'm sorry ma'am, it was just-"

She laughed "I'm kidding. You're too adorable for you own good." I might have been inclined to be agree with her if she wasn't 5'9, a red head, in possession of the curviest hips known to man and didn't have a face crafted by the gods. Certainly not stiff at all.

Instead I smiled tightly "I had no idea."

She turned to me; a curious expression covered her face then something else before it was covered with a smile "Who might you be?"

"Suzy, this is Ryan my boyfriend. Ryan, Suzy is assistant editor and my boss." Jason quickly introduced us. I shouldn't have been this nervous. Jason was obviously gay and very much involved with me. But there was something about her that told me to remain on my guard that I shouldn't sit too easy with her.

"Pleasure. I love your magazine." I replied.

Suzy smiled "I'm always glad to get feedback from another happy customer. Now if you'll both excuse me, there are some things to oversee." She took her leave. I was relieved.

"You ok?" Jason asked.

"I'm   fine."   Was   my   ever   cheerful   reply.

Things are weird with Astrid.

Why does Ryan feel uneasy about sweet Jason's boss? Comment and vote to motivate me if you want to find out.

Chapter 25

S ONG - PRISONER - THE WEEKEND FT LANA DEL REY

"Do you know she's won like three journalism awards?" Jason tumbled another fact about Suzy. I handed him the plate of chicken chow mien and even gave him more spring rolls because I knew how much he liked them. But it was dropped on the coffee table in favor of more talk about my boyfriend's boss. He had been rather charmed by everything about her therefore Suzy Spielberg had now become one of the main topics of our conversations for three days straight.

It was always about how cool she was, or how she didn't let the models boss him around like they did with the other photographers or how considerate she was with his adjustments and didn't turn it down like most of the editors. Or how she'd worked for the big papers before settling down in fashion as it was her main dream. Or how she was a hardworking woman who still had time to raise a family.

Basically, she was all the good things on earth wrapped in one blonde package.

I clenched my teeth each time.

"Sounds great babe." I mumbled stuffing a spring roll into my mouth.

"And she's just like ten years older than us!" He exclaimed. "That's a real achievement."

"Must be." I echoed.

The TV was muted showing an old episode of Game of Thrones. Cersei's face appeared cool and calculating as ever. I couldn't even enjoy it if I wanted to. Not when Jason couldn't stop worshipping his freaking boss.

"Her husband is some hot shot on Wall Street who didn't want her to work but she still defied the odds and went after her dreams." He continued.

"Wonderful." Another spring roll roughly shoved its way into my mouth with so much force it was a miracle I didn't choke.

"It's amazing how they're rich enough for her to stay at home and watch the kids like a typical housewife but she's so talented and can't-"

"That's all great." I cut Jason off from his ramblings. He blinked surprised "Are you ok Ry?"

I stabbed my food so hard that a little plastic end of the fork broke into it "I'm fine. Just a little irritated."

"Irritated?" He repeated after me. "But why? Did I do something?" damn his naivety. I sighed "It's just that you've been talking non-stop about how awesome your boss is for the past few days. I get it, she's a great person but please lower it a notch? Most times it feels like you'd rather be on a date with her than me."

There it was out. But three days of hearing about the amazing Suzy Spielberg had set me on the edge.

Jason raised his eyebrows. My last comment may have come out a little rawer than I'd anticipated but

"I didn't realize how much I'd been talking about her. I'm so sorry about that."

"It's ok." I replied. It wasn't.

He took my plate from my hand dropping it next to his before taking my hands to face him completely.

"I'm sorry." His voice was deep, strong and warm. My annoyance was already peeling away bit by bit. "It's just that I'm new and still a bit nervous and she's done so much to make me feel welcome there."

More than enough I'd say.

"Unfortunately it's delved a little into hero worship but the last thing I want to do is get you angry." He explained gently and goodness I wanted to remain mad at him forever. "I'll tone down my work talk then."

"I don't give a fuck about your work talk. I just really wish you would stop talking about her." I said bluntly in a bid to get him to see my point.

"She's just really nice. It's not my fault that whenever I talk about work she comes up because she's my supervisor and boss." Jason added unhelpfully. The anger I thought was forgotten came rushing back. Had he not heard me at all?

I narrowed my eyes "Well then go have dinner with her. She can probably suck your dick later instead of me." Throwing my chopsticks away, I stood up from my position on the floor, trotted to my bedroom then slammed the door hard enough to make something rattle.

I knew that I was overreacting. There was nothing going on between them. My boyfriend was obviously as gay as they came. But coupled with the still lingering presence of Chris' visit and the unpleasant revelation that I had fallen into old habits with my vomiting, my emotions were all over the place. I didn't want to be the needy boyfriend who wanted attention all the time but somehow I did want our time spent together to at least be focused on only us.

Between school, hanging with Astrid or Jay and being with Jason, he always distracted me best. A distraction was well needed.

Chris had called me about two days previously when his school trip was about to leave the city. I didn't answer the call but instead let it go into a voicemail that I listened to.

I lay down on the bed wrapping my hands around myself with a grunt. My entire being felt heavy. It was strange. Everything was supposed to fall in place by now. But I felt less secure than I did previously. It appeared as though reminders of my past that I had so desperately wanted to stow away began to pop up.

I didn't want to go back to that time when I hated Chris more than ever.

Nor did I want to remind myself what it was like to jam a finger down my throat just to get by.

Those should have been behind me.

They were behind me.

A faint knock disturbed my train of thought. With a hum against my pillow, I spoke "Come in."

Jason entered hesitantly leaving the door open "You sure?"

I closed my eyes "Come in or get out."

The door indicated its closure with a click. My eyes remained shut so that I could pretend I didn't want to know what Jason was doing. His socked feet shuffled on my carpets until I felt a pair of arms envelope around my waist pulling my backside towards his warm body. I refused to shiver when his lips grazed the shell of my ear "I'm sorry."

No answer.

"I should be more sensitive your dislikes and likes. Suzy is a good person but I don't need to keep reinforcing it with you. It's rude."

No answer.

"She's just my boss. I don't have the hots for her, god forbid it. There's only one blonde I'm interested in." my treacherous body pressed itself closer to Jason once the hardness of his pants found its way to my butt. He slowly traced his lips from my ear down to my neck placing tiny kisses. My own pants began to tent forward.

"You can't seduce me into accepting your apology." I finally let out blocking a moan.

"I'm not." His innocent tone was masked with something lecherous. It was mind blowing how sweet Jason managed to be but in the bedroom he became a completely different monster. A sexy talking, manipulative and risqué monster. My favorite.

"Don't you dare sass me. I didn't say I hated it." I replied tilting my neck to give more room.

"Ok then." Jason said delightedly in-between pecks.

My eyes fluttered "That doesn't mean I'm not still mad at you. I feel like you don't pay attention to me sometimes. I don't want to be that nagging boyfriend."

"I do. I'm sorry for making you think that." I held back a moan when he went at my erogenous zone with his teeth. This man was not playing fair.

"Oh baby." This time I couldn't hold back a moan when Jason flicked his tongue down my happy trail. "I get jealous the way you talk about her and I hate it. I shouldn't feel insecure but I do."

All movement completely stopped making me face my boyfriend in semi frustration. But Jason had sobered up at my confession "Ryan I didn't know that. I didn't mean to make you feel that way."

I sat up to properly face him placing a hand on his cheek "I know. That's just my own issue not yours."

"Not entirely. I should have realized that talking excessively about my boss was making you upset." He was clearly upset with himself. I smiled "You're not a mind reader Jason. Not like you could have really known. I know that I shouldn't feel that way but sometimes I guess it just sneaks up on you." not to mention the fact that a part of me still felt ugly and useless. It didn't matter that Suzy was woman. To me all she represented was another beautiful entity with access to Jason who had the power to snatch him up the moment he realized that I wasn't good enough.

"Ryan I love you. Please don't ever feel insecure or unsure of your place in my life. You're at the very top I swear." Jason pleaded.

There was no reply from me.

"She's not you. I love you." he emphasized.

I nodded "Thank you for that reassurance. I needed it."

"Are you ok now?" Jason asked.

I shrugged "Not sure. I'm still horny as fuck since you're such a tease."

He grinned "Well we better remedy the situation then."

About two hours later Jason was snoring naked beside me. His arm was carelessly draped along my torso and our legs were entwined together. I couldn't sleep. My body was sore and worn from the thorough ravaging I'd been through but my brain just couldn't shut off yet.

"Jason?"

He snored in reply, dead asleep. I counted to three before throwing his arm off me and grabbing my purple robe discarded on the ground. Jason moved to hold my pillow to replace the absent body. I quietly grabbed my phone and walked to the kitchen. Feeling thirsty, I filled a glass with water and gulped it down in literally two seconds. Enjoying the relief the cool water gave; I moved to my wine cabinet and opened a fresh bottle of red wine.

I didn't even bother getting a wine glass and drank straight from the bottle. Much better. I scrolled through my phone going to the voice mails until I reached the particular one that I was interested in.

Ryan....it's me Chris. I'm the last person you want to hear from and I guess that's ok. I'm more than deserving of your hatred. I'm not calling to ask you for an apology but to say that I truly understand now. Whatever happens to me, I deserve it. I accept it. I'm just so sorry that I put you through all of that all those years.

My fingers were shaking.

Right now I'm standing here and I don't even know what to say. I'm sorry Ryan, I'm not trying to apologize but I'm just sorry for everything. You deserved a better sibling than me. You're a good person despite all you think and I regret all that I made you into.

Made me into? My brother was taking responsibility for his part in my undoing.

Don't forgive me. It's better that way. I don't deserve it. Goodbye Ryan.

The voicemail ended.

Chris said he finally understood what he had put me through. It made me wonder, was my brother gay? That was obviously not the answer. Dad called several times to fondly complain about my little brother making out with a particular girl in the living room. It was possible that he was hiding it and using the girl as a beard, but my mind told me there was something else.

Something else was plaguing my brother.

The question was; did I want to find out?

Did I still care about my baby brother?

Another question; what the hell was it aboutSuzy Spielberg that made me uneasy?

A storm is brewing.......

How would you guys feel if I told you this story would soon come to an end?

Chapter 26 (Greendale)

This chapter will contain triggering content.

SONG - WALL F*UCK - FLUME

"Ryan Michael Perry. Tell me where the hell you got this wrist watch from." Mom demanded. I shrugged "I don't know."

"Be serious and tell me where you got it from." Her patience was thinning. Too bad I could barely give a crap. It was my mistake to forget the watch that Gerald had given me in my pocket. When the clothes got sent down for laundry, Mom found it and that was how the shit storm began.

"Where did you get it?"

"I bought it."

"Bullshit." It spoke volumes about the level of her anger if she was able to carelessly swear "This thing must be worth hundreds of dollars. Where would you get that kind of money?"

"Working at the ice cream shop downtown."

"Don't make me punish you." she threatened.

"Do your worst." I challenged.

"What's going on here?" Dad waltzed into the confusion in the laundry room. Mom angrily let it all out "I found this watch inside his pants and it's clearly not his. I've been asking your son for the past twenty minutes but he's refused to tell me a word. I don't know how the hell he got it or if he-"

"If I what Mom?" I cut her off. "Stole it? Trust me that would be the least of your worries."

"Well I don't know what to think." She snapped causing Dad to cautious hold her arm. I had no real problem that my mother had found the watch. I didn't care. I'd shut her out of my life in such an unreal way that we'd almost become strangers. It wasn't as though we were close in the past. With my previous pains and sorrows it was easier to cling to my Dad because he understood better.

Mom may have tried to understand me. I didn't notice it if she did. What I did notice was that she didn't really have the skills to remain as patient as I needed. It certainly wasn't a walk to in the park raising an outcast of a son.

Dad tried to intercede "Ryan, I think it would be better if you tell us where you got it." His voice was gentle, pleading. I could never deliberately disappoint my father. He was my rock. My protector. Yet I desperately wanted to let him understand that this wasn't about him, it was about Mom.

In my pain, I desperately wanted to hurt her. Draw it out and start a fight. Push her to the very edge she'd been too careless to stop me from reaching.

But I couldn't lie to my father in the end "My boyfriend gave it to me."

Cue the gasps. Dad remained patient; his shock was well hidden "Oh. Who is he?"

"You don't know him." I mumbled. I hoped that they would never, considering the fact that I wasn't playing around with just one person.

"I realize that now. He gave this watch to you?" Dad asked.

I nodded "I'm not lying."

Mom mumbled something. I glared at her "Right, of course I'm lying, because you can never think anything but the worst of me."

"Ryan-." Dad tried to soften the storm.

"No Dad, it's true and you know it. I'm her one and only disappointment." Each word was a bitter vial in my mouth. It hurt. Just because it was true and I had accepted it didn't mean that it was easy to accept. None of it ever was.

"You never tell me anything." she tried to defend.

" 'Cause you don't care." I shot back.

"That's not true. I didn't even know you had a boyfriend." Mom interjected soberly.

"There are plenty of things about me you don't know." I snarled finally storming out of the laundry room. Chris was in the living room watching TV with bored eyes. He looked curious at my angry speed walk but tried to look away in fear that I would turn my anger towards him.

Apparently that had become the new normal.

"Where are you going?" He risked once I grabbed my car keys from the rack in the hallway.

"Out." My answer was curt.

"It's late. Mom and Dad will get mad." He warned. I stuffed my phone into my pocket before turning back "Wow you're so smart. Great observation." Satisfied with my brother sinking into the couch solemnly, I darted out of the door and into my car. The keys dropped from my shaky hands twice before I was able to place it into the ignition and turn it on.

There was no destination in mind when I started driving. I just wanted to leave. Go far away. Cry for a definite length of time. Unfortunately, it seemed as though I couldn't do all these things at the same time. I parked my car on the side of the road because the tears made my sight blurry and I couldn't see. Despite my state of mind several months ago, I didn't want to die.

My life had just begun, according to Astrid.

I sighed turning off the ignition and lazily draping myself over the steering wheel. I was exhausted – both mentally and physically. Gerald Coffey had turned himself into my invisible body guard. He always hung around wherever I was as subtly as he could. It was very annoying. The man had all but declared his undying love for me.

It had gotten harder to meet with Emmett much to his irritation.

Stringing the two males along became more work than fun. It wasn't a game anymore. I didn't know what I was playing at. When Nathan confessed that his reason for making my life hell was as a result of his sick feelings repressed, I thought it would make revenge sweeter. It seemed sweeter. But lately I couldn't find it within me to care.

A future out of this toxic town was what had taken space on my mind.

Nathan avoided me like the plague when I was in school. It was a relief. Lately I'd begun to think that my need for revenge was useless. Nathan and Emmett had hurt me terribly in the past. But I was a new person now.

I could finally leave and forget it all. There would be no need to carry it around with me. I wasn't going to obviously forgive them but things would certainly be easier if I let it all go.

Certainly since the boys had become exhausting.

A knock on my window startled me. I looked out to see Nathan. Not the person I was expecting. At all. A moment of brief fear past before I unwound the window glasses "Can I help you?"

"Yesss." He slurred. He was drunk. His face was sweaty and his front hair was matted against his forehead. His eyes turned around. The front door of his flashy car was flung carelessly open on the main road. He was really drunk. Probably from some stupid party. He'd gotten too tipsy to drive anymore and just stopped on the road.

Fate so had it that it turned out to be right where I was.

"That's dangerous." I commented on the position of his car.

"Don't give a fuck," Nathan proudly proclaimed.

My heart beat quickened "What do you want?" he leaned closer sticking his head into the car. I felt the urge to step on the pedal and drive out of the area as fast as possible. But my body didn't cooperate. I was tired. I was scared.

"I tried to stay away." For a moment I thought he'd sobered. "I tried but y-you're just there. I can't stop wanting you. I need you. Please stop this. Stop doing this to me." No, no not this again. I thought it had ended. I thought it was over.

I tried to stay calm "What do you want Nathan?"

"You." He whispered.

Before I could do anything, he opened the door of my car and tried to yank me out. I hit his harm "What the fuck?! Let me go!"

Nathan growled stumbling back, clutching his arm in pain "You fucker."

My action had fueled even more anger into him. I tried to shut the door but the alcohol seemed to quicken Nathan. He tore off my seat belt dragging me outside. I struggled against him but he was strong enough to hold me down. He twisted my arm to his convenience "Leave me alone! What do you want from me?!"

He was almost emotionless, robotic "Make it stop."

Before I knew it, my body slammed against the car "Leave me! Stop it! I'm begging you stop!"

It was in that horrific moment I understood what he wanted. He was going to rape me. He was going to take it to lengths I'd never imagined.

He was finally going to take everything from me. Tears feel down my cheeks as I felt him fiddle with his pants "Please. Please stop."

My voice was hoarse. Painful. I couldn't breathe. I wanted to die.

Just die.

"If I do this, it will all stop." Nathan whispered against my neck. I cried hard, wishing my life to end right in the moment. But luckily for me.

Nathan never got far.

In a staggering moment of strength, I elbowed him making him startle backwards and fall unto the asphalt. He groaned in pain but I couldn't care less. If I was lucky he'd hit his head and bust it open. With barely any time to feel relief, I jumped into my car turning on the ignition and driving way with my pants still loose against my waist.

I was in a trance. For a moment it felt as though I'd been dreaming. Did it just happen? Did I dream this whole thing?

No, it was as real as could get. Tears poured from my eyes and I sobbed with everything in me. What had I done to deserve this? Why couldn't I be happy? Was pain destined to be my only companion?

Destroy, my inner voice whispered, Destroy them all. The anger is your friend. Use it and destroy all who hurt you.

Suddenly my head stabilized. I calmed down. It didn't hurt so much anymore. My tears dried up. My heart hardened. I knew exactly what to do.

If I needed a motive for revenge, this was a perfect one.

So that happened. I actually wrote that. Wow.

Hell hath no fury like Ryan scorned.

Chapter 27

- -

S ONG - THIS IS WHAT IT FEELS LIKE - BANKS

Strangely enough, I hated Christmas in New York. In Greendale, I didn't fancy it either but it was more indifference than anything. When I was younger I loved it but growing up became a different case. Gone was the magic and wonder of the most special month of the year; it's replacement was that Christmas had simply become the second holiday in a year that I was allowed to eat whatever I wanted without (some) guilt.

But moving to New York, I hated it for different reasons. As early as November, the major stores and shops would start putting up signs and decorations. Most people started shopping early on before the retail craze began.

During the second week of December, it became a fully mad thing. Almost everywhere you went Christmas carols were blasting around. Some cheeky carolers would come out to screech annoying renditions of holiday classics (oh Boney M how you've suffered). Red and white streamers were every-where along with ridiculous Merry Christmas neon signs.

Then the pressure to buy Christmas gifts for people would mount on my shoulders.

Each year I sent presents to my family since I never went home for the break. The only person I'd ever really looked forward to see was my Dad but he couldn't leave my Mom and Chris home just to come and visit me.

My avoidance was a known fact but not one any of us acknowledged. Mom pretended like she didn't know how much it agonized me to call her at the end of each month, acting like we were on good terms rather than the strained individuals we both knew we were. Dad acted like my refusal to visit home was some prolonged hiatus and not because I surely would be burned on a stake the minute I stepped into town.

They knew what I'd done during my senior year before bolting to college, yet it was never spoken of. Just another incident swept under the rug.

In a way I should be grateful. With no one to make me remember, it was one less memory that allowed me to sleep better at night.

Over the past few years, that had slowly become my own personal motto. Forgot your actions and pretend they never happened.

That must be how murders live with themselves.

"The two of you are being extremely unhelpful right now," Jay commented at Patrick and me. We were both draped lazily on one of the short couches in the clothes store where he had dragged us to go shopping. He and Patrick were hosting a dinner party for the holiday which would consist of Patrick's co-workers and some of the guys at NYU where Jay and I went to. Therefore, it was decided that Jay needed a new outfit for the occasion and as his boyfriend and best friend respectively, Patrick and I were forced to come along.

"You look good. Like you've looked in the past ten outfits," I said exasperatedly.

He rolled his eyes "I'm going to try the next one," Then disappeared back into the changing room. Patrick took the opportunity to sigh "He's like this every Christmas. Holiday crazy."

I grinned "Well you're going to endure it for the rest of your life so no use complaining."

He sighed but I could tell he didn't care "Like the past four years haven't told me anything."

Jay jumped out of the dressing room wearing a grey sweatshirt "How's this look?"

"Beautiful," Patrick said with a dreamy look. Jay wrinkled his nose "It's just a shirt babe. Don't get a boner." But he was cleared endeared by the compliment. I pretended to gag "As wonderfully disgusting as this is, I'm bored and hungry so speed up the process."

"Why so testy? Hasn't Jason been fucking you well enough?" Jay teased.

I rolled my eyes "No he has. That's the reason I'm so cranky. He fucked me against the windows at my apartment thrice last night. My ass is sore which is why I'm testy. I've had good sex but no food." My statement was true. When Jason came home from work, he made no sport of lifting me up from my spot on the couch and mounting me against the windows for the entire city to see.

Before then I had no idea that voyeurism was a thing for me.

"Did not need to know that," Patrick muttered while his boyfriend laughed. I smiled "But no kidding, I feel like my stomach is going to burst open if I don't get any food in it."

"Shouldn't that be the opposite reaction?" Patrick asked confused. "I also find it strange Ryan that you're hungry and you didn't even hit one clothing store."

I yawned "That'll be much later. Today's for telling Jay how good his ass looks in new jeans."

"Plus Ryan's too posh for us. He doesn't shop anywhere that isn't Burberry or Chanel," Jay teased. My reply was simply a half-smile. There was no need to tell him that it'd probably have to cool it down until I graduated and found a decent paying job. Strangely, I wasn't even upset at the prospect. My mind was far too excited thinking of when Jason and I would finally move in together after I finished college.

I yawned again "A burger sounds heavenly right about now."

"Chill out. I'll get you some Mickey D's when we get out of here," Jay offered.

I sighed "That would be really lovely."

While munching on French fries, I noticed how intimate Jay and Patrick were. They were feeding each other food, giggling over Coke and ending each of their sentences with endearments like "babe" "honey".

It was quite nice to know that they'd gotten over their issues. In the past such a show would have made me squirm then make up an excuse to leave early, but now I didn't mind much. Jason had definitely softened me. The concept of a normal relationship had slowly wormed itself into my heart. I was comfortable with movies nights and burnt curry. I loved waking up to his alarm then tossing it in annoyance. I even loved finding his socks amongst my laundry. I especially loved getting a text that didn't make me sigh out because I thought my current partner was being too clingy.

Jason was all the right kinds of clingy.

He was the right kind of everything period.

My spin still stiffened at the mention of love. It was still a foreign concept to me. But lately, it seemed to be something I could gradually find myself easing into.

I could actually see myself falling in love.

I could see myself falling in love with Jason.

"Uh oh. He's smiling to himself. I think we've got a crazy white boy in our hands babe," Jay broke me out of my thoughts.

Patrick actually giggled "He looks crazy doesn't he babe?"

I pushed my tray forward "I think someone slipped something into your food. I'll go walk around in hopes that this will turn out to be some crazy hallucination." They both waved me too busy playing with each other's lips.

On my way out of the McDonald's section of the food court, I noticed Patrick slap Jay on the butt to which the dark skinned boy reacted by giggling.

I power walked away from the area.

With nothing else to do, I walked around aimlessly in the mall. Several shoppers passed by me rushing to get their desired items before everyone else got them first. I stopped by the candle shop seeing that they were having a sale on organic soy candles. Buying some for Astrid didn't seem like a bad idea. The girl had quite a thing for candles; for a while I thought she was pyromaniac.

Sadly she was in Vermont for Christmas with her mother before she would go back to Denmark to end the holidays with her father next week. I missed her. We were always buddies when it came to Christmas shopping.

My present for Jason had been acquired a few days before. It was wrapped and hidden in the safe in my bedroom because I was too nervous that he would find it. I imagined how his face would look on Christmas Day when he finally unwrapped it.

I shook my head; no use getting too excited before then.

"Ryan?"

It was Cornelius. He stood by the door of the candle shop with a bag signifying he'd purchased something.

"Oh wow. We always met up in retail places don't we?" I laughed nervously.

He smiled "Must be our thing then."

For some reason I felt the urge to bolt as fast as I could away from the spot. Instead I remained frozen in place "Shopping for Christmas?"

He looked down at the bag "Oh yes I suppose. Although this is more for me than anyone else."

"Huh," I said stupidly "Candles are nice."

"They are," He repeated. We were both silent for a while until he broke it "There's no need for this to be as awkward as we're making it you know. Plenty of people bump into their exes all the time."

This time a more genuine laugh bubbled out of me "Ha, more like almost ex. We didn't stay long enough together to actually get to that point."

Cornelius let his smile whither "Of course. How could I forget?"

I swallowed acknowledging how my statement must have hurt him "I'm sorry for all of it though. I really am."

He shook his head "Don't apologize for something you can't control. It perhaps was never meant to be."

"That doesn't mean that you aren't a great guy," I tried to convince. "For the short time, you treated me right. I'll always be grateful for that."

Cornelius had a wistful expression "Perhaps in another life."

I shrugged "Maybe. Life in unpredictable in every manner." But in this particular life I was glad to be with Jason. He shuffled around on his feet "Does that mean we can't still be friends?"

I pursed my lips "I don't think that would be such a good idea."

"Come on," He cleverly tried to persuade "You can't really think that there's no chance for friendship because we went on one date?"

No, I wanted to say, there's no real chance because you're clearly infatuated with me. A stony faced couple walked past us and into the store. I sighed "Maybe. We'll see." I didn't just want to rule him out with feelings. He'd been there for me when Jason and I had my break. Even if it was in his own way, he did comfort me.

Cornelius was right, we could be friends. There was nothing wrong with that. If he could keep his feelings at bay, then there would be no problem.

It could work.

"What do you say," His voice was charming and sweet and everything that could drop any living being to their knees "Friends?"

"Yeah," I echoed shaking his outstretched hand "Friends."

Chapter 28

P repare for waterworks people...

SONG - PRETTY WHEN YOU CRY - LANA DEL REY

"Have I told you how much I hate knotting ties?" Jason grumbled out. I hid a smile and shrugged "Not really. It's not like you've been lashing about it for the past ten minutes. My boyfriend made a displeased noise at the back of his throat "I don't even know why we're doing this. We should just stay home, order some take out and watch Orphan Black."

I refused to let my heart flutter at the suggestion of such a domestic scene.

"Babe, it's DIAMANDIS magazine's Christmas party. You can't miss it," I reminded him while simultaneously patting my own outfit in the mirror. Since Jason was their new contract photographer he'd been given an invitation to attend. As his boyfriend, I was his plus one. Throughout the day I made sure that my outfit was good enough if I wanted Jason to show me off perfectly. The possibility of upstaging Suzy Spielberg had nothing to do with it.

Jason frowned "Don't remember that being stated in my contract. Attending all work related functions is a must or else your pay will be docked."

I smiled at the playful comment "But still it's not a bad idea. Isn't there going to be lots more people than the magazine staff and executives?"

"Yes."

"Wonderful. This is your chance to network babe. You get meet lots of people with the same interest as you. Friendships are made and opportunities provided. Who know maybe you'll get other contracts and even an audience for when you decide to open your own private showing," I explained to him.

Jason smiled pleasantly "I never thought of it that way. You're right babe. Good to know I have my very own business major guru."

"I'm an engineer first and foremost," I pretended to be annoyed. "Business is my minor."

"Hmm either way you're mine," He muttered sucking my neck. My eyes fluttered "Glad we can both agree on that."

"Yes," His hand creeped underneath my blazer. I pushed it away "Babe we have to be there in fifty minutes. No time for messing around."

"But I'm horny," He whined.

"Not an excuse," was my stern answer but my boyfriend was persistent. He moaned in my ear pressing his bulge against my ass. I bit my lip trying not to give in but it was too much. My hand swung around to push his head closer to my neck "Stop Jason."

Jason made no move to do so. In the end I gave in and let him have his way with me. We were late to the party but I don't think anyone really cared.

It was at the Plaza Hotel. The DIAMANDIS Christmas party was in full swing. Models, Designers, Photographers, Writers and everyone else who mattered in the fashion were all gathered. Jason had been apprehensive to leave my side but I encouraged him for his sake. There was no crime in wanting my boyfriend to succeed in his field. From my spot behind the pillar I watched him in satisfaction.

Jason was a shy creature but having him talk about his passion made all the difference. The flute of champagne in my hand tasted sweeter just watching him go.

I was proud.

Very soon it wouldn't be just DIAMANDIS seeking him for contracts – all the major magazines would want him. He might not even want to work for anyone then once his private showings became public envy. I had such high hopes for my boyfriend.

It was foreign sensation to care about the success of anyone apart from myself. Jay and Astrid were my friends so their success obviously brought me joy but not in the way Jason's did. There was nothing I wouldn't do for him, I thought fiercely.

"Are you alone?" A fairly attractive man in a suit asked me.

"Not at all," I answered sweetly.

"I find that hard to believe. Your girlfriend mingling?" He asked.

I curled my lip "Boyfriend. And yes he's mingling quite well." The man hummed "What a shame. He must be quite careless for leaving you alone here by yourself." I knew exactly where this was going. I had to nip it right in the bud.

Luckily it was that moment Jason looked away from the woman he had ben chatting with and gave me a bright smile. I couldn't even help my own smile if I wanted to.

"I doubt that. Excuse me," I didn't wait for a reply before making my way to Jason. "Jason, are you ok?"

"Wonderful," He beamed. "Your suggestion was great. I've talked to two photographers from the Royal Institute of Arts and a few models who agreed to model for me. My portfolio could be expanding since I'm looking to add a human element."

I nodded "That's awesome."

"It really is," He said softly. "So glad I took your advice."

"I do give the best advice," I boasted.

He kissed me right on the mouth surprising me a little. "What's wrong?"

I glanced around red faced "We're in public."

"So?" His eyes contained that reckless abandon I adored so much. "I don't see anyone stopping us."

I giggled "Careful there. Your boner is showing." Before it could go any further, Suzy appeared. Shark-like smiles, bright red lipstick and all.

"Suzy," Jason cleared his throat "I haven't seen you all evening. I'm glad you invited me to attend."

Suzy laughed "Ah please don't be silly. You're practically family here at the magazine. Oh I see your boyfriend managed to attend."

My smile was as tight as they came "Happy to see you too Suzy."

Her smile tightened too "Same Raymond."

"Ryan," I corrected with a tilt of the head. Jason didn't seem to notice our exchange "I'm glad this night has been a success so far."

"It has," Suzy said "Oh by the way Jason, Mr. Yates has been asking for you. He's been particularly impressed with this months' cover and wants to see the individual who created it."

"Really?" Jason piped excitedly. Simon Yates was the owner of DIAMAN-DIS magazine. A stamp of approval from him was pretty much the same as earning of the approval of all the Fashion deities.

"You should go," I encouraged. Of course I didn't want to be left alone with her but I didn't want him to lose an opportunity because of my jealous urges. He kissed my cheek beaming "I'll be back soon."

"He's a mild force of nature," Suzy commented on my boyfriend's retreating form.

"He's going to do great things," I replied.

She hummed "I agree. That's why I think he needs all the opportunities he can get. No distractions, especially not from any of the dead weight in his life."

I froze with my glass mid-way to my mouth "Excuse me?"

"I believe in assets not liabilities," Suzy continued "To achieve success, useless things must be left behind where they belong." The nerve of this woman. Was she implying that I was nothing but dead weight in Jason's life? It was a surprise that my flute didn't shatter with how hard I'd been clutching it.

I sighed to control my rage "You're right. I'm happy to inform you that the only thing my boyfriend has are assets. I've made sure of that."

"Really?" Her expression was amused.

"Yes," I replied curtly. "Excuse me."

Another second near this woman and I would do something utterly drastic without a thought. This was all for Jason. I couldn't ruin it for him. Not when he'd worked so hard just to get this.

For the next hour I made myself scarce. Mostly because I was still sulky at what a bitch Suzy had been. There was something she was out to get, I was sure of it now. If it was Jason then tough luck for her because he was mine for the time being. Even if he wasn't, there was still no chance for her. Speaking of my boyfriend, there had been no sign of him for the past hour.

Feeling a little testy and a lot bored, I went to the bathroom to freshen up before I went to find Jason and convince him to let us go home.

Only the sight that greeted me once I entered told me that that would be happening any time soon.

I must have been dreaming.

No I was dreaming.

There was no way to tell, especially since my sight had become more blurry than clear in just three seconds. It was as though time had stopped leaving me with nothing but the sound of my chest shattering to pieces.

Jason leaned against the wall, eyes closed and delirious while a twink knelt right in front of him, giving him the blowjob of a lifetime.

"Jason?" I whispered.

"He's busy." The man on his knees smirked. Jason said nothing; he was drunk and utterly useless. My body felt numb all over. I couldn't feel a thing. My chest contracted.

I needed to breathe so badly.

Yet I didn't dare take in a single gulp of oxygen.

I guess at the end of the day, he did drop his dead weight.

My hands were cold as I walked up to the steps of the unfamiliar house. A few weeks ago I wouldn't have even dreamed of being here but as I'd noted a few hours ago, dreams had a strange way of shifting within a short period of time.

I knocked twice, afraid that I would be turned away. I couldn't have my heart broken twice in one night.

I wasn't physically capable of handling it.

I was barely able to handle myself as it was.

I knocked once more. A tall man around his late sixties wearing a suit who I assumed was the butler answered the door "Who are you?"

"I want to see your boss," I answered.

He blinked "I'm sorry-"

"Just tell him that Ryan is at the door," I said tiredly. The man hesitated but went inside closing the door on my face. I stood there for about ten minutes waiting, fearing that he'd just left me without relaying my message.

"Ryan?" Cornelius appeared.

I breathed in relief "Hi."

Epilogue

This literally the shortest epilogue in history.

SONG - STOLE THE SHOW - KYGO FT PARSON JAMES

"Ryan," Jason tried.

I packed up the last of my boxes into the taxi "Please don't." a part of me wanted to feel bad at the state of him.

It was a sunny day. Paloma's Authentic Restaurant was open and they still sold the best damn tacos I'd ever tasted. I got my tacos from there the first day I met Jason.

We also went there for our first date.

It was right there he handed me that last box of things I'd left at his place.

"I swear it wasn't my fault. I don't know what happened." He tried to plead.

"So your dick just fell into his mouth?" I asked sarcastically.

He was helpless "I was drunk. I swear I don't remember anything."

"That makes it all better doesn't it," I threw the last one into the taxi. "This is was all obviously a mistake. I'm the one who should be sorry."

"Ryan-"

"Sorry it every happened," I continued "Sorry that I was stupid enough to believe that we were something meant to be. The time for believing fairy tales is over."

Jason was on the very verge of tears. I forced myself to look away so that I didn't get the urge to comfort him. My mind flashed back to that moment when I first discovered him and that guy in the bathroom during the DIAMANDIS party. He was so out of it, he didn't even recognize me. The offending guy on his knees had an alarmed look on his face but it died down the minute I didn't react.

All I did was stand there for about two minutes before I closed the door. The first person I bumped into was the man who tried to hit on me before.

"Leave me alone!" I shouted before he could utter a word.

Leaving everyone who'd heard me flabbergasted, I stormed out of the event hall. That was when I went to Cornelius's house in the Upper East Side. I'd known his address previously but never visited him before. I didn't think I would ever want to.

"What are you doing here?" He asked carefully. I was still in the clothes I'd worn to the party. It was 2am in the morning. On my face were dried tears and red rimmed eyes. I was an obvious mess.

"If you're still interested," my voice was sorrowful, firm "I want what you offered me in the beginning. I want a deal. I fuck you and you give me money, clothes and all the works. Whether you decide to add those things you said at the mall, it's your choice. I've told you all I want. Are you still interested?"

Cornelius paused "I do. I still want you."

"Good," I muttered. "Now I'm yours." He didn't waste time before pulling me into a crushing hug.

There was no such thing as love. I'd been right in the very beginning. Love is fake. Love is a useless dream. Love had done nothing but tear me down and left the pieces to rot.

Love was the sweetest poison and it had ruined me.

"I trusted you," a tear drop fell from my eye. "And you betrayed me."

Jason was fully crying now "I know but I swear that I didn't mean to. I don't know what happened."

"Stop saying you don't know!" I shouted. Angrily wiped the tears from my face with my sleeve "You were there! He was blowing you and you were there! How the fuck can you claim not to know?!"

He sobbed "I'm so very sorry Ryan. I love you and I'll always love you. I messed up, I swear I don't know what happened but I love you."

I closed my eyes "Love? Love is a joke. Nothing but a big fat lie we tell ourselves because we can't stand being alone. You don't love me. You never did."

"I do," He whispered. I entered the taxi "Goodbye Jason. I wish that I never met you."

The taxi sped off leaving him behind on the sidewalk. I didn't make it thirty seconds into the ride before I burst out in tears once again. "Damn young love," muttered the cab driver.

Milton Keynes UK
Ingram Content Group UK Ltd.
UKHW021833060724
445042UK00014BA/748